UPSTANDER

UPSTANDER

JAMES PRELLER

Feiwel and Friends
New York

A FEIWEL AND FRIENDS BOOK
An imprint of Macmillan Publishing Group, LLC
120 Broadway, New York, NY 10271

mackids.com

Our books may be purchased in bulk for promotional, educational, or
business use. Please contact your local bookseller or the Macmillan Corporate
and Premium Sales Department at (800) 221-7945 ext. 5442 or by email at
MacmillanSpecialMarkets@macmillan.com.

Library of Congress Control Number: 2020919105

First edition, 2021
Book design by Mike Burroughs
Printed in the United States of America by LSC Communications,
Harrisonburg, Virginia
Feiwel and Friends logo designed by Filomena Tuosto

ISBN 978-1-250-25152-7 (hardcover)

1   3   5   7   9   10   8   6   4   2

This book is dedicated to all the Jonnys in our world,
and to the people who love them.

1

[gravel]

PLINK, TICK, TICK. IT WAS RAINING IN MARY O'MALLEY'S dream. Soft water splashing rhythmically somewhere. Or summer rain tapping against glass.

No, not rain. Handfuls of gravel tossed against her second-story bedroom window. Dragged from her dreams, Mary reached for her phone on the floor beside her bed. The time read 3:27.

She rolled over, rubbed her eyes in the darkness.

Down below, Jonny tossed another handful of small stones scooped from the driveway. They tapped like buckshot against the aluminum siding. For a star athlete—correction: a former star—his aim wasn't what it used to be. High as a kite in the dark of night. Locked out again.

Mary went to the window, looked out, and there he was down below, back arched, hands on his hips, looking up. And it *was* raining, as a matter of fact, a soft August drizzle. From Mary's vantage point, her older brother, her only brother, looked like a lost boy. Small and soaked and, in this case, shirtless and razor-thin. Why *isn't he wearing a shirt?* All ribs and pointy elbows, he smiled goofily, performed a daffy, loose-limbed shuffle, and acted out a nearly incomprehensible pantomime. Mary knew what he wanted. She could lip-read as he mouthed his request: *Let me in.* Didn't apologize, didn't ask. Maybe he thought he was cute. He probably wasn't thinking much at all. The old charmer had attempted to enlist Mary as his co-conspirator. *Well, that ship has sailed, dear brother. Now you're just annoying.*

Fed up, her mother had taken to bolting the front door, a desperate move that didn't quite make sense to Mary. Her mother's boyfriend, mild Ernesto, didn't get involved in Jonny's antics, kept a place two towns away. He might have been here that night or maybe not. But Mary couldn't leave Jonny out there, and never would. It was the same old dance. The small, fractured family all playing a game of pretend.

Careful not to wake their mother, Mary tiptoed downstairs, slipped back the lock, and opened the door. Jonny swayed a moment, then reached out to steady himself against the doorjamb. His head lolled gently, his eyes unfocused, his skin pale gray in the lambent light, and he offered Mary a two-fingered salute. "You're a lifesaver," he said before he stepped dreamily into the house. "A cherry, berry, raspberry, snazzleberry . . ." He dropped the thought as he reached the stairway landing, caught himself with a grip on the railing, and began the great ascent. The effort required more focus than he was able to muster. Mary walked behind her brother, her outstretched hand shadowing his movements, ready should he fall. Jonny clomped and lurched and climbed bent forward at the waist, murmuring almost inaudibly, leaning heavily on the railing, giggling softly, sometimes pausing for long moments before taking the next step. Mary followed her brother down the hall and stopped at the threshold of his room. Jonny had already forgotten her, stumbled through, pushed the door half closed, left her behind.

They would not speak of this, ever.

On her way back to her room, Mary noticed the light leaking from beneath the door of her mother's bedroom. She was up, had undoubtedly heard it all. Probably had been sitting up on the edge of her bed, brain blazing with worry. Mary climbed into bed, reached for her phone, sent her mother a text: *He's home.*

Her mother had replied instantly: *k.*

Minutes passed. Mary rolled, flipped her pillow, strained to hear sounds in the silence of the house. What she wanted to hear was beyond her capacity, the sound of air pushed past lips, the liquid thrum and swoosh of a heart pumping in a room down the hall of this house of secrets. So Mary rose and went to her brother's room. She pushed open the bedroom door. It was too dark to see, so she flicked on a closet light, opened that door a few inches, the weak light spilling across the carpet. Jonny was sprawled on top of his bed, designer sneakers still on his feet. He hadn't bothered to crawl under the covers. Dead to the world. Zonked, stoned, high, toasted, wasted, whatever. She approached him, bent down, and listened: ah, he's alive. Mary felt an urge to kiss him on the cheek. She brushed damp hair from his face. One arm, his right, was extended out and hung off the bed. She untied his shoes, rolled the socks off his feet. She found an afghan in a sailor's trunk at the foot of the bed and pulled it over her brother's bruised and ravaged body. His jeans were slung low, beltless, half falling off his narrow hips.

When did all this happen? When did she become the caregiver and her nineteen-year-old brother the hapless, helpless, damaged child? Mary yawned. A sad story, years in the making. It had been happening long before Mary realized it. Jonny in trouble at school, injury, pills, depression, rehab, relapse, promises and broken promises, tears and accusations and more drugs. Always more drugs. Where was it going to end?

Oh, how she hated and loved him so.

Mary drifted back to bed, and soon merciful sleep shut her eyes. Good thing it was summer. She could sleep in as late as she liked, dead to the world.

2

[triangle]

THE SEARING AUGUST SUN STREAKED THROUGH MARY'S
bedroom window, bringing the room to a low simmer.
Mary felt muzzy, the sharp edge of a headache pressing behind her eyes. The air-conditioning had never
worked right in the upstairs part of the house, and
she'd forgotten to pull the shade. So hot and stuffy
and gross. These were the days Mary was grateful
for her budding friendship with Alexis Brown and
Chrissie Saraynan. It had been the summer of lounging by Chrissie's pool, wearing cute bikinis, eating
carrot sticks and chips, relaxing in the sun. And if
just sitting around ever got boring for Mary, if the

conversation ever felt tedious, she'd simply lower herself into the water by the side of the pool. What else were you going to do in the hazy days of global warming? If the planet's going to cook, if we're all gonna burn anyway—might as well get a killer tan.

Chrissie had one of the nicest houses in town, three stories with two white columns. The backyard was deep, with a grassy area fenced off for the dogs—they owned two huge Irish wolfhounds, Ani and Aram—backed by a large area for the pool, bluestone patio, and curtained pool house, complete with bathroom, outdoor shower, and full-size refrigerator. Once the girls settled back there, they never needed to enter the main house, which Mary guessed was probably the idea. So in sequence: sidewalk, house, dogs, pool. Beyond the pool there was a six-foot stockade fence that separated private property from the playing fields of the local elementary school. Yeah, Chrissie's family had money.

Chrissie and Alexis came conjoined as a perfect pair, so it had been a surprise for Mary to find herself invited into their inner circle. Thanks to Mary, the third point on the plane, the girls now formed a triangle. Mary knew from math that there were different types of triangles: isosceles, equilateral, scalene, obtuse, others. It had to do with distances and angles, where the points sat on the plane in relation to one another. In a perfect triangle, there would be three congruent sides with three angles of sixty degrees each. Human triangles were never, ever perfect. Mary's relationship with Alexis and Chrissie, she decided, formed an acute triangle. Their points were close together, tightly connected by a short line, whereas Mary's point floated off into space like a flickering star. This didn't bother Mary in the slightest. The reality simply matched the way she felt inside. Alone and shining in the distance.

Throughout elementary school, Chrissie had been unremarkable. Generally unnoticed. Well-dressed and wealthy with nice stuff but never, at least to Mary's mind, particularly interesting. She'd been gangly and awkward, arms and elbows jutting out at pointy angles. Nobody ever looked twice. Until, suddenly, in the autumn of sixth grade, they did. Boys and girls both. And it was widely agreed that Chrissie Saraynan had blossomed into a rare flower. Her eyes were dark and heavy-lidded, only ever half-open, giving off a sleepy expression, as if she'd just woken up or was about to doze off. If anyone asked, Chrissie would say with startling certainty that she planned on becoming an actress after getting a nose job and dropping out of college. No one doubted it would come true.

Alexis had come from a different elementary school, so her history was less known to Mary. Where Chrissie could be aloof, almost regal, Alexis was the girl everyone wanted to be. Athletic, smart, confident, and pretty in a non-boring way. Alexis had, it must be said, the most amazing mouth. It was a little too big for her face, too wide, too full, giving her an almost alien quality. But also, undeniably, it was a mouth made for kissing. Sensuous, soft. Judging herself against Alexis, Mary hated her own thin upper lip and felt like the dullest dishwater in the world.

On this particular afternoon, a fourth girl, Chantel Williams, was also present, altering the group's geometric shape. Mary wondered whether it turned this afternoon's group into a trapezoid. A rhombus? Certainly not a parallelogram, with equal parts. Or maybe that was it: Chantel and Mary were the equal, short, slanted lines. Supporting players. In any event, that might be how the trouble between them started. Bad math. The numbers weren't right. Chantel was dark-skinned and solidly built, though people often stressed the point, when Chantel was not in earshot, of saying how pretty she could be if only.

If only she'd figured out what do with her hair.

Or lost ten pounds. Okay, fifteen.

And got some new clothes. Something less last year.

Or just tried harder.

Because, again, she had such a pretty face!

Great eyebrows! Amazing eyebrows!

If only.

3
[interlopers]

CHANTEL HAD THE IDEA THAT THEY SHOULD PLAY
something, not just sit around, so she brought along a
game of Whoonu. Despite Chantel's enthusiasm, and
the fact that Whoonu was actually a decent game in
Mary's (unspoken) opinion, Alexis wasn't much interested. She had veto power, able to alter a day's plans
with a stifled yawn. After some desultory discussion,
they decided on Monopoly. As far as Mary could
tell, Monopoly was the default game after everyone
had run out of actual good ideas. The compromise
that nobody wanted. So they got out the board and
started the game. Everyone understood that they'd

never finish and nobody cared who won anyway. It was just something to do until something better came along.

"This feels so BC—Before Computers," Alexis groaned, giving the die a half-hearted roll.

"Park Place! Want to buy it?" Chantel, the banker, offered.

"I suppose I should," Alexis said, counting out the hundreds. She picked up her phone, tapped a few times, smiled, and showed it to Chrissie.

"Oh God, what a dork!" Chrissie laughed.

Mary observed it all with mild irritation, still tired from her interrupted sleep the night before. "Let's take a break from the game," she suggested. "Anybody want some chips? They're onion ranch."

At that moment Mary noticed three heads peering over the fence. Three boys, wide-eyed and grinning like hyenas. "Hey!" she shouted sharply, pointing in the direction of their peeping admirers.

Heads turned and the boys ducked out of sight.

"That was Griffin Connelly!" squealed Chrissie, jumping to her feet.

A moment later Griffin's head popped back up.

"It's like a million degrees out here," he said. "And that pool looks so nice."

"Tough to be you," teased Alexis. She turned and whispered something to Chrissie. "Who else are you with, Griff?"

"Hakeem and Cody," Griffin answered. "Hey, is that lemonade? We are literally dying of sweat out here. It's gotta be a hundred degrees."

"Dying of sweat?" Chantel said to Mary. "What does that even mean?"

Hakeem and Cody hoisted themselves up, stepping on a couple of cinder blocks they'd dragged to the fence. "It is super hot," Hakeem said, wiping the back of his hand against his forehead.

"Yep, yep, yep," Cody chirped in agreement. "Roasty toasty."

"Are you staring at the pool—or spying on us?" Alexis teased.

Griffin grinned, tilted his head from side to side. "What can I say? It beats looking at these guys."

Chrissie laughed. Chantel crossed her arms.

"Should we invite them over?" Alexis asked in a whisper. "What do you think, Mary?"

"I don't know—" Mary began.

"Please!" Griffin pleaded in a faux hysterical voice. He was cute, no doubt about it. Mary didn't know-know him, but she was aware of Griffin Connelly. Everybody was. Griff was one of those boys with a brash, boisterous, full-volume personality, always seeking attention, usually surrounded by a group of friends. It was impossible not to notice him. As far as she was concerned, Griffin Connelly didn't know that Mary existed.

Mary would soon find out she was wrong about that.

4

[connection]

THE BOYS PLAYED LIKE SUGAR-AMPED CHILDREN AT A birthday party, just goofy kids not pretending to be anything other than what they were. Their splashy playfulness, to Mary, was as refreshing as the water itself. She hooted in appreciation as the boys made ridiculous dives, cannonballs, belly whoops. Hakeem dug out a rubber football from the pool house, and that led to elaborate games on the diving board, full of fabulous catches, screaming, and lots of showing off.

They were loud, and lively, and Mary considered them a happy distraction on an otherwise dull day. Griff, of course, was the natural leader. And by far the most charismatic, though not, to Mary's surprise, a particularly gifted athlete. He was slightly awkward, unpracticed. Cody was a live wire, skinny and sinewy with an unpleasant face. The teeth, the nose, the eyes—the proportions weren't quite right; it was all off-kilter. Hakeem was the one. When he leaped off the diving board, he performed effortless flips and twists. After sitting as spectators with Chrissie and Alexis, Mary and Chantel finally answered Griff's tireless requests—"Come on, we need you!"—and joined in. Chrissie and Alexis lounged contently, unmoved by the din, sipping cold lemonade through plastic straws.

Mary prided herself on her ability to throw and catch a football. Skills developed after many games of touch with Jonny. Her brother and his pals—the old gang that never came around anymore. Mary laughed to herself, remembering it, how they used to call her brother Jonny Football. He was really good. When was that? She counted back the years. He was nineteen now, last played as a sophomore, so he was sixteen when he mangled his knee, had surgery, and lost interest. She had to have been around nine years old when last horsing around with a sports-obsessed brother she adored. Yeah, Griff, that's where those tight spirals came from. Catch!

For this game, the quarterback stood at the shallow end in waist-high water. The receiver waited on the diving board one meter above the water, bounced, bounced again, and jumped off as high as possible. The quarterback tried to time the throw just right, hit the leaper in the belly with a perfect pass. Catch and splash. They kept score—boys always needed to keep score—and they shouted and laughed and called each other hilarious, insulting names. Usually at Cody's expense, though he didn't seem to mind. Just grinned and said, "Yep, yep, yep." Weird kid.

Miraculously, pizzas arrived and were devoured.

Hakeem and Cody settled in to a game of cards with Chantel. Griffin plopped down between Alexis and Chrissie. The trio—a new triangle?—did a lot of scrolling, laughing, making and posting seven-second videos, looking over shoulders to see one another's screens. Griffin tended to press close. Flirtatious, touchy, predatory. Mary wondered if Griff liked one of them, or if it even mattered to him which one. Mary grew restless. She wanted to draw something—she'd been carrying around a sketch pad lately, and a new set of colored pencils—but wasn't about to do it with the guys around. "I'm getting changed out of this wet suit," she said to nobody and drifted toward the pool house.

When she emerged, Griffin was there. Like he was waiting for her. He made a point of acting like he was watching the card game, standing off to the side and commenting, but Mary knew better.

"Hey," he said. "You know, we have a connection, you and me."

"Yeah?" Mary raised an eyebrow.

"Your brother sometimes hangs out with my sister, Vivvy—or used to. I'm not sure anymore, since she got an apartment in town with a couple of friends," Griff said. "I don't see her much."

"Jonny?" Mary said, as if there was any other brother.

"Yeah, I met him a couple of times. Funny guy. He used to come over to our house. My dad works the second shift, so . . ."

Griff let the sentence fade out.

"Vivian Connelly," Mary said. Maybe she had

heard that name before. She wasn't sure. Her brain was glitching out, a malfunction in the software.

Griff leaned close, whispered, "I heard he spent a few months at Western Winds. Did it work?" Western Winds was the name of a private hospital that specialized in what was officially described as "teen mental health" issues. A place to go if teenagers or young adults were showing signs of depression, got caught doing too many drugs, screwed up with the law, attempted suicide or even considered it. Basically, if you were a kid and your life went off the rails, your parents sent you there for a tune-up. To get things back on track. Sometimes it worked. High school graduation, college, maybe a summer in Europe, a good-paying job: success.

It helped Jonny for a little while, and then it didn't help at all. Like a vacation that was amazing until real life kicked in and you forgot it ever happened.

Mary didn't know what to say. Her mind clouded over, shut down. She shook her head. "This conversation isn't happening. I gotta go," she said, and moved past him.

She hated that Griff knew.

"Hey, don't be like that," he said.

Her family's business was a secret. It wasn't something to chat about while snarfing down pizza and chips.

What was it Griff had said?

They had a connection.

No, Mary thought. *No, we don't.*

5
[marshmallows]

WALKING HOME, MARY RESOLVED NOT TO THINK about Griffin Connelly. That boy had jangled her nerves. *We have a connection.* Yeah, right. She looked forward to popping a marshmallow—or, okay, three— into her mouth. Not at the same time, of course. Eating marshmallows always helped bring her world into balance. *Namaste*, Mary thought, grinning to herself. She imagined a chubby marshmallow, with little stick arms and legs, doing yoga. Downward dog, maybe, or meditating. That might be funny to draw. Ohmmmm. If she could think of a clever caption, it might even be a cartoon: the mindful marshmallow.

Mary kept a secret stash of marshmallows in the back of her bottom dresser drawer. The big, extra-fat ones they sold at Stewart's for s'mores. Marshmallows were Mary's weakness. But, seriously, that wasn't the best way to express it: a weakness. It's not like Mary wolfed down an entire bag in one sitting. It wasn't a problem; she wasn't in a marshmallow crisis or anything. Mary knew that sugar was super bad for you—everyone saw the same videos in health class—but a couple a day wasn't going to kill anybody.

Mary then made the strategic mistake of opening the front door. Home sweet home.

Her mother's voice came from the kitchen, sharp and urgent, "Are you high right now? Just tell me."

"Jesus, Mom, no!" Jonny shot back.

They were fighting again. It felt as if the air in the house was crowded with charged particles. Mary could sense the electrons and protons ricocheting off the furniture like steel balls from a shotgun. The muscles in her lower neck tensed.

"You're lying—" her mother shouted.

"Hi! I'm home!" Mary called out in her sunniest voice. It was as much a plea as a greeting: I'm home; you can stop now, please. Mary heard the rattling of dishes in the sink, the scraping of a chair across the floor, but no greeting in response. She waited, slipped off her sandals. *This is ridiculous*, she decided. *I'm in my own house. I live here.*

"If you love me, you'll stop." It was her mother's voice, raw with emotion.

"I told you. I'm not using," Jonny retorted.

Mary stood at the entranceway to the kitchen. Her mother leaned against the counter, arms crossed, scowling. Jonny sat at the table, cereal floating in a bowl of milk. He wore an unbuttoned cardigan sweater. Yes, in August. The rules of this particular contest: no punching, no kicking, just words. Winner takes nothing. Jonny tapped a spoon in agitated rhythm on his right thigh. That was his giveaway. The way his eyes darted and his body vibrated with pent-up energy. The muscles of his jaw tightened from clenched teeth.

"Don't come in here, May," Jonny warned, not looking in her direction. "Mom's acting like a crazy person again."

There was a prickly edge to his voice, like razors strung across wire. His hair looked oily and uncombed. His pale skin appeared nearly translucent, except for the dark circles under his eyes. Mary thought, *Don't pretend I'm on your side. I'm not your ally, brother. I'm not on anyone's side.*

"I don't even recognize you anymore," her mother said. "This isn't you, Jonny. It's not you."

"Oh, Jesus, here it comes," Jonny muttered, the spoon rat-a-tat-tatting against his leg. He raked a hand through his hair.

Mary's mother stepped toward her only son, palms open. "You've got to listen to me, Jonny. We can't go on like this."

Jonny flicked the spoon into the cereal bowl, splashing the milk. The spoon bounced and rattled to the floor, hitting his mother's leg. "I'm trying to eat one bowl of cereal in this insane house," he roared. "So freaking what? I slept late. Lots of people do. Besides, I have a stomachache. It hurts. I probably have an ulcer. Do you even care? Besides, what temperature do you keep it in here? I'm freezing!"

"It's set at seventy-two degrees—"

"It's too cold. I get the chills living here. It's ridiculous, Mom. I'm nineteen years old. I party a little bit. A regular, normal amount. It's one of the few things in the world that actually feels good. That's my big federal crime, Ma? That I go out with my friends?"

"Your friends," her mother scoffed. She brushed the thought away with a wave of her hand.

"Yeah, my friends." Jonny rose to his feet, his movement sudden and alarming. "Real people who actually care about me."

Mary stood paralyzed, watching it all. They had forgotten she was there. She had become invisible in her own kitchen.

Mary's mother stepped back. She brought a hand to the side of her head, trying to collect her thoughts—or to keep them from exploding. With obvious effort, she adopted a softer voice. More soothing, calmer. "Jonny, please, listen to me. Please. You need help. I think you have a prob—"

"Oh no. No, no, no. I'm not going back to that place," he said.

Her mother held out a hand, patting the air. "Okay, okay, just . . . sit . . . okay?"

"You can't make me. I'd rather die than go back to Western Winds," Jonny replied. He sat back down. Swiveled his head, stared coldly at his sister. "Good luck when I'm gone," he said. "It'll be just you, Mom, and the Garden Gnome in this demented house."

The Garden Gnome was Jonny's nickname for Ernesto, their mother's boyfriend. Ernesto was short and paunchy, and he wore a scraggly, elfish beard. Not his fault, but those were the facts. Mary stifled a grin. She caught herself and flashed a time-out sign with her hands. "Stop. Just stop."

Mary crossed to the refrigerator. Grabbed two clementines, checked her phone, looked from her mother to Jonny. "I'll be in my room," she announced. "Headphones on."

6

[ghosts]

ON DAYS LIKE THIS, MARY HATED BEING HOME, AND most days were like this. The house full of drama, worry, stress; her mother anxious about Jonny, and Jonny doing whatever he pleased. The same tug-of-war nearly every day. Threats and accusations followed by excuses and broken promises. Which was why Mary spent most of her time outside or up in her room, drawing pictures, painting, eating marshmallows, zoning out.

It was the summer when Mary first realized she lived in a house of ghosts. One by one, they'd started moving in, replacing the old occupants. Their father was the original ghost, but he had passed years ago, when she was only three, so that wasn't new or, for Mary, keenly felt. Jonny was the big change. The thing with ghosts is when they take over, they don't send out a group message. It's subtler than that. You might not notice the change for weeks, months, maybe years. Then you look up and, oh wait, "You're not my brother."

"Yes, I am," the phantom replies.

But you both know it's a lie.

The real brother has vanished, maybe gone for good.

The ghost stands there, lanky frame swimming in an oversize T-shirt, wearing his clothes, pretending to be her beautiful big brother.

But it's totally not.

Mary could tell by the eyes, darting from place to place: the floor, the window, the bedroom door, as if scanning for exits in case of fire. Ghosts are weird about sleep. They don't need much of it at night, but then will nod off at the breakfast table, a half-chewed piece of raisin toast in their mouth. It's the ghost way of eating. Food doesn't really matter to them; swallowing was part of the disguise.

She heard Jonny clomping in the hallway, coughing. It didn't sound like he was being followed by their mother, which was a good thing. Sometimes she chased him up the stairs, and the battle raged on and on. Maybe they declared a ceasefire. The bathroom door opened, then closed. She heard the shower.

Mary swung open her door, left it partly ajar, and returned to her desk. She spied Jonny as he padded past like an old cat, towel wrapped around his waist. He was skinnier than ever, ribs showing, scapula blades too prominent, but somehow having him home felt less dangerous than the thought of him out there somewhere, doing who knows what. Home, at least, he was safe. That was the dream anyway.

The thing with ghosts, Mary speculated, is they don't feel anything. That's how they know they're dead. The not-feeling is a big clue. It's also helpful, because that's basically how a ghost tolerates being a ghost. Because, again, the not-feeling thing. The last sensation a ghost wanted was to start feeling emotions, empathy, self-awareness, anything. That was how Jonny lived now, she could tell. It was like when your foot's fallen asleep and then you try to walk. Zombie foot. Those pins and needles, fighting against the numbness.

The only way you wake up is through pain.

Ghosts want to stay numb.

They don't want to feel—because feelings hurt.

For some people, maybe even her brother, drugs were novocaine for the soul. As the dentist says before he sticks in the needle: "You'll feel a slight pinch, and then it won't hurt a bit."

Mary scribbled in her sketch pad. Weird faces inspired by Picasso, ears where eyeballs ought to go, cockeyed expressions, twisted lips, dangling noses. Then she looked at the page in surprise. Shock, actually. For across the bottom she had scrawled the words, *Is he going to die?*

Mary's mind didn't consciously pose that question. It was as if her hand had dreamed it up, the worryfear rising up from her body.

So, well, is he?

Mary sat and stared, pondering the answer. She almost added, *Maybe.*

"We all die, May," Jonny had told her once. He'd called her that for years, changing Mary to May. She called him Jonny Bear—for no particular reason. She liked their private nicknames, their secret language. She recalled that conversation, we all die, the one time she got up the nerve to confront him with her deepest fear: that he might be killing himself, that he'd ruin his life if he wasn't careful. Get off drugs. Stop altogether. Come back to being Jonny, the brother she'd lost, the one who had abandoned her when she'd needed him most. After Mary's big speech, all those passionate, carefully rehearsed words, that's all he had said. Smiled wanly in her direction, like a poser Holy Ghost, as if he knew a secret but couldn't tell. "Everybody dies. We all die, May."

She could have punched him in the face. Should have. Because at that moment it felt to Mary like he was already dead. Already lost, adrift, floating tetherless through interstellar space—where no one can hear you scream. Mary felt forsaken. The core experience of being abandoned began when her father died in that car accident. She didn't have many memories of him. At least, not true memories. There were photographs, videos, so she knew what her father looked like, how he acted when the camera was on, but it didn't seem completely real to her. A memory of a stranger once removed. Horrible to say, but her father might as well have been a supporting actor in a movie she saw at the Cineplex 18. Their father's death was harder on Jonny, though he never said much about it. No complaints. He just pulled up his socks and went forward with his life—and he was pretty fabulous for a long time until, all at once, he wasn't so fabulous anymore.

Now it's their mom, Patti, and this latest boyfriend Ernesto—who was perfectly fine in a lumpish, who-really-cares kind of way. Mary kept her distance. She couldn't tell if Ernesto was for real or not. Here to stay or just passing through, eating all the good snacks. All her life, it had always been Mary and Jonny, together. Not aligned against their mother, exactly, but definitely #TeamKids. And then Jonny ghosted them all.

Mary heard a shout. She lifted the headphones away from her left ear.

Her mother was screaming up the stairs.

Jonny's door slammed.

Give it up, Mom, Mary thought.

Give up the ghost.

She turned up the music, loud, but it never got loud enough.

7

[pic]

MARY LIKED CHANTEL, AND THEY WOULD HAVE HUNG out more if Chantel wasn't so incredibly overbooked. Where Mary enjoyed long stretches of free time, Chantel always had something to do: sports, clubs, music lessons, Girl Scouts, household chores—even a mini job as a mother's helper, caring for a neighbor's eight-month-old baby. Chantel never had downtime. It left Mary feeling sorry for Chantel—so scheduled!— and also a little envious. So it came as a refreshing change of pace when Chantel invited Mary over for quesadillas. "My travel basketball practice got canceled, so I asked if I could invite a friend over,"

Chantel explained over the phone. "We could watch a movie, too, if you want."

Chantel had three little brothers that she good-naturedly referred to as "the monsters." They were lively and cute: Darius, Jamel, and Keyon, though Mary wasn't completely straight on who was who. Mr. Williams was away in France traveling on business, so Mary and Chantel helped Mrs. Williams prepare dinner. Even the boys had jobs. They set the table and filled water glasses without grumbling.

Mrs. Williams was one of those "involved" parents who asked a lot of questions. Not nosy, but Mary could tell that Chantel's mom was probing to get the lowdown on things. Mary did her best to present herself as likeable and friendly, that was one of her talents, except she wished she had a better story to tell. No, no father; no, not playing sports; no, my brother dropped out of college; no, we're not planning any trips this summer; and so on. Maybe she should make things up? Invent a more interesting life. *Yeah, played with baby elephants in Kolkata, India. Super fun!*

After dinner, which included ice cream and prayer and salad (but not in that order), it was bath time and story time and every other kind of time Mary could imagine. "Getting the monsters to bed is a big production around here," Chantel offered with a smile. Mary helped Chantel clear the table and put the dishes in the dishwasher.

Chantel's phone buzzed. She glanced at it and shook her head. Mary sensed the message had upset Chantel, because she grew quiet and had a faraway look in her eyes. Suddenly, Chantel held out her phone and said, "He keeps asking me to send a picture."

At that moment, Mrs. Williams entered the kitchen. Chantel hurriedly pocketed her phone. "It looks great, girls, thank you. Mary, you are welcome to stay if you'd like. I believe Chanti had her hopes on a horror movie. I'd be happy to drop you home if you can't get a ride."

Mary looked at Chantel, who smiled and nodded.

"That sounds great, Mrs. Williams. I'd love that!" Mary replied. "Thank you very much."

Mrs. Williams pointed two index fingers toward the ceiling, reminding Mary of an old Western gunfighter. "Listen, I've got the three amigos up there. Jamel and Keyon are in the tub. I have no idea on

God's green earth what Darius is up to. I think he's building a Lego space station or alien prison or some such folderol." She waved a hand, amused by it all. "We haven't had any drownings yet, and I'd like to keep it that way."

"I can help—" Chantel began to offer.

"No, Chanti, you entertain our guest while I wrestle those rascals into bed." Mrs. Williams made a loud *whew* sound, as if she was exhausted, but her eyes told a different story. They twinkled brightly. Maybe she didn't mind all that mothering after all.

The girls didn't pay close attention to the movie, except for the really good parts. They'd both seen it already. Instead, they huddled close, sharing one light blanket, and talked.

"Who is asking you for a pic?"

"Hakeem," Chantel answered, her voice barely above a whisper. "Promise you won't tell. It's so stupid."

"Of course," Mary said. She paused a beat. "What did you do?"

Chantel craned her neck to make sure her mother wasn't nearby. "I didn't even understand him at first," she admitted. "I was like, a picture of *what*?"

Both girls cackled.

"You didn't, did you?" Mary asked.

"No!" Chantel answered. But after a pause, she admitted, "I didn't say no, either. I made excuses like, 'I'm busy' or 'I look bad right now.' You know?"

Mary nodded. She didn't know, she'd never been asked before, but it was exciting to think about. Mary wondered if Hakeem had asked Alexis or Chrissie. Some boys were like that. She'd heard that older guys collected pics of girls and swapped them like trading cards. It was pretty gross. But also a little flattering. Like it might be nice to be asked by the right person, even if the answer was still definitely no. Some girls said it was no big deal, that sharing a photo was the new first base.

"I like him," Chantel said. "Hakeem's nice and funny and—

"—kind of good-looking," Mary added, exaggerating slightly.

Chantel let out an embarrassed laugh. "I guess, yes. But he keeps asking me. 'Send a pic, send a pic. You look so good.' All that stuff. Persistent, you know? I'm afraid if I shut him down, he'll stop talking to me."

They both stared at the movie for a few minutes.

Someone was getting stabbed with scissors. "Lupita Nyong'o is so beautiful," Mary said, admiring the actress on-screen.

"I know," Chantel agreed. "Her skin is perfect."

"Boys can be such idiots," Mary said.

"Are they all like that?" Chantel asked.

Mary shrugged. She didn't know. "It seems like a lot of them are, maybe. Like it's normal for them."

Chantel shook her head. "He says the pictures fade away after seven seconds . . ."

"Yeah, but they can take screen captures," Mary warned.

"Hakeem keeps saying he's not a screenshotter," Chantel said. "And you know what? That makes me think he is. If I sent him something, he'd have it forever."

"Yeah," Mary said. "And who knows what he'd do with it after that."

8

[family]

IT WAS ONLY AUGUST 9, BUT MARY HAD STARTED thinking about "back-to-school" clothes. Maybe it was the brainwashing from all those commercials that played incessantly, but still: Mary's wardrobe could use an update. Some jeans that fit right and a couple of soft sweaters would go a long way. A new pair of boots would be awesome, she knew the exact ones she wanted, but Mary wasn't going to push it. Her mother had promised to take Mary shopping soon, but soon never came. It was natural for Mary to compare her home life with Chantel's. Three little hilarious monsters compared to one brother who had become pretty monstrous—and not in a cute way. Mrs. Williams was so good at being a mom. Kind and happy and fully present. Meanwhile, Mary's mother was always anxious and preoccupied. Mary knew for a fact that her mother constantly stalked Jonny on social media. It was like her full-time mission. Sherlock Mom. Every time Jonny tweeted or posted anything, Mrs. O'Malley was there, clutching her phone, scrolling, stabbing her fingers at the screen. She did everything possible to keep tabs on where he was, who he was with, and what he was doing. As far as Mary could tell, it didn't make one bit of difference. Jonny was either out getting zonked or home, zonked out in bed. A college dropout, he worked part time at McDonald's and hated it.

That night, Mrs. O'Malley made a special meal of chicken and penne with vodka cream sauce. At precisely seven o'clock on Friday night, dinner was served. Everyone was in attendance, even Jonny and Ernesto, who was dressed in a bright orange polo shirt, black hair combed back, white walking shorts, high white socks and brown loafers. It was a look.

Mary could tell that her mother was more tense than usual. Mrs. O'Malley was halfway into a bottle of red wine, and she displayed a jittery cheerfulness that felt forced. Like a hamster running in a wheel, screaming, *THIS IS SO AMAZING! I'M RUNNING AROUND IN A GIANT WHEEL!* Yeah, right.

"It's so nice to all be together like this, isn't it?" Mrs. O'Malley announced.

"It smells delicious!" Mary said, ever cheerful. The good child. Murmurs of agreement all around. Even Jonny mouthed something positive.

During dinner, Mrs. O'Malley worked valiantly to inspire some form of conversation. She prodded and asked questions and talked about new shows on Netflix that she had heard about from coworkers at the bank. Ernesto told a confusing story about work—he managed a car dealership out on Sunrise Highway— and Mary answered questions about how her summer was going. "Fine, good, a little boring," etc.

Jonny didn't say a word. Just sort of grumblingly sat there, moving food around with his fork.

"You're not eating, Jonny," Mrs. O'Malley noted, perhaps with a little too much edge. "Don't you like it? I made it especially for you."

Jonny stabbed a piece of chicken. "I'm eating," he said.

"Well . . ." Mrs. O'Malley faked a laugh. "I'm looking right at your plate."

"It's very tender," Ernesto chimed in.

Jonny lifted his head. Staring straight at his mother, he brought the chicken to his mouth and made an exaggerated show of chewing it. After swallowing, Jonny ran a napkin across his mouth, took a sip of water, and echoed Ernesto in a louder voice—"It's very tender!"—set down his fork, pushed his chair back, and started to get up.

"You've barely touched your meal," Mrs. O'Malley said.

"I'm full," Jonny said. "Besides, I'm going out tonight. I'm going to need the car."

"Sit," Mrs. O'Malley said. She summoned a smile to her face. "I mean, please, stay with us for a few minutes. Don't rush off this instant."

Jonny squeezed his eyes shut and scratched ferociously at the back of his neck. He nodded twice, as if making a decision. Plopped down in the chair. Mary noticed that his right leg started to bounce. It was a nervous habit that had gotten worse lately—sewing machine leg. Up and down, up and down, up and down. Too much nervous energy. Jonny sat there, fidgeting, a live wire. "Isn't this nice," he said, looking around from face to face. "The happy family."

Ernesto rose to get a beer from the fridge. "Need anything, hon?" he asked.

Mrs. O'Malley shook her head.

"I cleaned my room today," Mary volunteered, hoping to shift the room's energy. "And the upstairs bathroom, too. Those scrubbing bubbles really work!"

"Oh, gee. Aren't you Miss Perfect?" Jonny mocked.

Mrs. O'Malley cleared her throat. "What happened to your guitar?"

"What?"

"You heard me, Jonny. I bought you a beautiful Martin acoustic guitar for your fourteenth birthday. It cost nine hundred dollars. You used to play it all the time."

She paused, looking tired and worn, and pressed on. "Where is it?"

9
[things]

JONNY COUGHED VIOLENTLY, POUNDED HIS FIST INTO his chest. He walked to the counter, spit grossly into the sink, filled a glass with water and gulped it down. Mary suspected he was stalling for time. "You've been going through my stuff?" he accused.

"I was in your room changing the sheets to your bed," Mrs. O'Malley said, not quite believably. She took a sip of wine. Placed both hands on the table to steady herself. "I couldn't help but notice that your guitar was gone."

"You couldn't help but notice," Jonny parroted.

"Where's your guitar?" Mrs. O'Malley growled.

Ernesto shifted uncomfortably in his chair. It looked like he wanted to disappear.

"My guitar," Jonny said, and again for emphasis, *"my guitar."*

"The one I bought for you, yes, that guitar."

Jonny gestured with his hands. "So that's how it is now? You go into my room, search through my things? Do I have to buy a lock?"

"I wasn't searching," Mrs. O'Malley clarified. "And it may be your guitar, but it's my house. My rules."

Mary shrank into her chair. She watched Ernesto take an unhappy swig from his beer. She wondered if it helped. If maybe beer had a magical quality that pushed everything off into the distance. Ernesto's gaze went to the ceiling. There was a frown on his lips. No wonder he didn't come around as much lately.

"This is bull," Jonny protested. "You gave the guitar to me. After that, it becomes mine. Why is that so hard to understand? And guess what? I lent it to a friend, okay? I wasn't playing it anyway. I'm kind of sick of it. The best musicians make music on laptops anyway."

"You lent it," Mrs. O'Malley said, obviously not believing him.

"Yeah, yeah, I did."

"To whom?"

"Oh, whom?" Jonny smirked. "Whom? Since when do you talk so fancy, Mom?"

"Jonny," Mary said, hoping to alter the path of their argument.

"Don't, just don't," he advised Mary, raising a hand like a school crossing guard. "I'm not in the mood for a gang-up. And especially not from my little sister. Stay out of it. I've got stomach cramps, my head hurts, the house is freezing, and now I have to listen to this." He looked to the front door like it was an escape hatch, ran both hands through his hair and snapped, "Can I have the car or what?"

"Honey," Ernesto murmured. "I don't think—"

"Oh, you're going to talk now?" Jonny said, turning to Ernesto. "I mean, wow, you're wearing a clean shirt today. You got your free meal. You can go now," Jonny mocked. "Besides, since when did anyone ever care what you thought?"

Jonny moved toward Ernesto, glaring.

Ernesto stared up at Jonny for a long, tense moment, his thick fingers lightly tapping the table. Otherwise the man sat perfectly still, like a Buddha or a coiled cobra. The threat of violence filled the room. Jonny was asking for it, almost begging for it, as if he desperately wanted to get the crap beaten out of him. The whisper of a smile appeared on Ernesto's face.

"That's enough!" Mrs. O'Malley demanded. She stepped between them and turned to stand toe-to-toe with her son. "You will not speak like that in his house. You will not treat Ernesto with disrespect. Do you hear me? This can't continue." She pointed to the front door. "We can't do this, Jonny. You've got to get help."

Mary sat quietly, her stomach churning. She felt lightheaded. It was hard to focus on anything. The room was spinning, swirling. She found it hard to swallow. How does that even happen? People swallow all the time without thinking about it. The body just does it. And now, suddenly, trying to swallow with total zen concentration was more than Mary could manage.

Jonny backed down, seemed to sag, looked at his feet. "Mom," he said in a whisper. "Don't."

"I think you sold it," she said. "That beautiful guitar. You loved it so much. This isn't like you. I'm worried, Jonny, and scared."

"Sold it?" Jonny replied. "Are you nuts? That's crazy. Why would I do that, Mom?"

"Money," Mrs. O'Malley said. She stared into the eyes of her troubled son. And then, in the softest voice she could muster: "For drugs. I believe you sold your guitar so you'd have money for drugs."

Jonny laughed, shaking his head derisively. He began to speak in a jittery, rapid-fire pattern of half sentences, forming a nearly incoherent symphony of anger and delusion. It struck Mary that he had snapped in some fundamental way. *Broken* was the word that popped into her head. His brain was broken. "Drugs, seriously? Okay, yeah, sure, I do need money—you don't help me at all!—I went through a rough patch with college, you know that, it was hard on me—I was depressed—and yeah, I didn't tell you, but I got fired from my job last week—it was soul-sucking, mind-numbing, and spirit-killing anyway—so don't even start with that—I don't have a father, by the way—that might have been nice—but even if I did sell the guitar, Mom, it's not a big deal. It's just a thing. An object. It doesn't matter. Why is everything about money with you? None of this matters," he swept an arm, taking in everything and everyone with one grand gesture. "Believe me, Mom. Where's your faith? It's not the end of the world. It was just a freaking guitar."

Mary poured water down her throat and it felt like drowning. She was all stopped up. It was hard to breathe. "I'm going out," she announced, rising. No one tried to stop her from fleeing. No one even asked where she was going. She wasn't even a blip on the radar.

10
[walking]

HE WASN'T ALWAYS THIS WAY.

Step by step, block by block, Mary repeated those words to herself: He wasn't always this way. Forcing herself to remember. She didn't think about ghosts or anything silly like that. This time it cut to the bone. Her big brother, who she adored since she was a baby, was turning into something horrible and ugly before her eyes.

Why couldn't he stop? It was drugs and prescription pills and alcohol. Mary didn't know what else he was doing, but she suspected it was bad. And getting worse. He didn't make sense anymore. His guitar! He talked gibberish, the story kept changing: He didn't sell it, he lent it to a friend, he might have sold it, nothing mattered anymore, and on and on. Jonny couldn't keep up with his own lies.

And since when did he become so mean?

How did Ernesto not crush him right then?

Mary walked without purpose or direction. Motored, really. Head down, tears in her eyes, fuming, muttering. She tried to remember the good times. Her real brother. Darkness fell without her noticing. She was in shorts and a T-shirt and sneakers.

An orange pickup truck juddered up, rolled along beside her. The passenger window slid down. "Mary? Mary?"

Mary shook her head, clearing out the cobwebs, and stopped. It was Ernesto. She should have recognized his truck; it had sat in her driveway many times. The guy loved the color orange.

"You all right?" he asked.

Mary stood on the sidewalk, bent at the waist so she could peer into the truck.

"I'm great," she stated in a flat voice.

Another car passed. Ernesto watched through the

front windshield, checked the rearview mirror. He looked at Mary and nodded. "Okay."

"She told you to come looking for me?"

Ernesto was silent. Shook his head once, a small movement. "I came on my own."

Mary almost smiled. He was actually a sweet man who was in way over his head. Ernesto reached across to push open the car door. "It wasn't easy finding you. Come on, get in. I'll give you a lift home."

Mary walked to the car and firmly, politely closed the door. "Thanks, really," she said, ducking her head through the open window. "I get what you are doing, and it's nice, but I need time alone right now." She stood, hands on her hips. There was a shaggy-haired boy seated on a bicycle, balanced on one leg, watching from across the street. Ernesto followed her gaze, turned his torso around to the left to get a good look at the boy. "Friend of yours?"

Mary nodded.

"Look," Ernesto said, "I need to get back there, in case your mother, she needs me."

"Is Jonny gone?"

"Yeah, yeah. He stormed out not long after you.

Broke the front hall mirror, though I don't think he meant to. Lot of emotions, lot of glass." Ernesto drew out the words with a weary sigh.

Mary made the calculation. Breaking a mirror was what, seven years bad luck? It also meant that her mother was alone—and probably freaked out.

Ernesto pulled a bill from his wallet, extended an arm outside the window. "Here's twenty. Get yourself a cone. Roberta's Ice Cream isn't far from here. I like the mint chocolate chip. Good milkshakes, too. Times like this, I'm a big believer in ice cream."

Mary accepted the money.

He looked back at the boy again, who still sat watching the car. "You sure about that guy?" he asked, throwing a thumb over his shoulder.

"Yeah, I'm good."

Ernesto flicked on the turn signal, pointed a stubby finger at Mary, and said, "You need anything, call me. You have your phone, right? You know my number?"

Mary started to shake her head.

"Listen, just text your mom. You call, I will come. That's a promise. Any time. When you're ready to come home, I'll come pick you up. All right?"

"Yeah, thanks," Mary said. "I just needed to get out of there."

Ernesto nodded, "Stay safe." He checked the rear-view mirror, put the car into drive, and pulled away.

Mary lingered on the sidewalk, watching the red lights of Ernesto's pickup fade into the distance. A breeze kicked up and she shivered. It was chilly for an August night. She glanced across the street at the boy slouched over his handlebars, still watching. She waved the twenty dollar bill in the air. "Woo-hoo! Twenty bucks! You like ice cream?" she called. "My treat."

Griffin Connelly pedaled over. "Well, that was weird," he said, blowing the hair from his eyes. "Sure, ice cream sounds good to me. But don't believe that guy about the mint chocolate chip. It sucks."

11

[roberta's]

MARY AND GRIFF SAT IN A BOOTH AT ROBERTA'S ICE Cream Palace—which was about as far from an actual palace as you could get. Still, the ice cream was sweet and creamy, and the space itself wasn't bad. There were booths along one wall, scattered plastic tables in the middle, and a long, low counter opposite the booths. It had a retro black-and-white tiled floor and fake rock star memorabilia on red walls. Everyone in town went there, especially on a Friday night in August. On any other day, Mary would have been reluctant to be seen eating ice cream with Griffin

Connelly—people might get ideas—but on this night, she couldn't care less.

Twenty dollars didn't buy much in the United States of America, Planet Earth, so they shared an extra-thick chocolate milkshake and a three-scoop Cosmic Crunch sundae. Mary threw the extra change in the tip jar. There wasn't much, and she didn't get a big thank-you.

Griff leaned back, swung his legs onto the booth bench, and groaned. "I'm stuffed."

They hadn't talked about anything important. Just ate, ravenously. Griffin gave Mary space, didn't crowd her with questions. She was grateful for that, and glad to have normal human company.

Mary leaned forward, peering closely at Griffin's face.

"What?" he said.

"You really do have incredibly long eyelashes," she observed.

"Yeah, I hear that a lot. My sisters are jealous." He shrugged and smiled in her direction.

"What were you doing out, just riding around?" Mary asked.

The shrug again, signaling *whatever*. "Actually, I was headed to Cody's. He's an amazing mechanic. Loves to take things apart and sometimes he even puts them together again," Griff said with a grin. "I was supposed to help him out. He's rebuilding a dirt bike, but I texted that I wasn't coming."

"That's neat, that he can fix things," Mary said a little awkwardly. *Neat*, how sad.

Griff nodded and looked away. He watched a group of high schoolers walk into the shop. Lacrosse guys and girls. Then he pulled his feet back around to the floor and said, "Do you want to talk about why you were wandering around with tears leaking out of your face? Because I can go either way. You don't have to. But if you want to," he said, looking directly into Mary's eyes, "we can do that."

"I wasn't crying that bad!" Mary protested.

Griff interlaced his fingers, stretched his arms toward the ceiling. "Okay, I'm not here to argue."

For the next thirty minutes, Mary babbled in a steady stream of words. She told him everything about what had been going on with Jonny, dating back a couple of years. The car accident—he claimed he got sideswiped in a hit-and-run—taking pills, quitting sports, his depression-slash-rehab stint at Western Winds, and so much more. But mostly, she talked about missing her brother. How that felt. Griffin was kind and sympathetic and a good listener.

Mary held her hands together in front of her chest, as if she were carrying a small bird that had fallen out of a nest. "When I was little, he used to come into my bedroom and read picture books to me. Or he'd make up his own stories—about brave frogs and a moose named Bruce!" She laughed at the memory. "I'd fall asleep listening to him. And every day he'd sing to me, 'Mary, Mary, quite contrary. How docs your garden grow?'"

"Wait, I know that one!" Griff held up a hand. He closed his eyes and haltingly said, "With silver bells and something-something smells . . . and the cow jumped over the moon?"

"Kind of like that, yeah," Mary said. The place was thinning out. The workers were wiping things down, the music had been turned up, a guy in a paper hat pulled out a mop. "I should really get home."

Outside Roberta's, which was tucked into a strip mall, Griffin said, "You should take my bike."

"What about you?" Mary asked.

"Ah, no worries," Griff said. "I actually don't live far from here, and you are, like, *pfff*," he waved a hand, "way out by . . . I don't even know."

"Magnolia Street," Mary said. "Not far from the middle school."

"See?" Griff said. "It makes sense. You take my bike. I'm good to walk. Seriously."

"I could just call home and get picked up," Mary offered.

Griff frowned. "Yeah, don't do that. It's better to be independent. Otherwise it's like you owe them something. Just take the bike, that way I know you're safe," he reasoned. "But you have to promise me something."

Mary waited. "And what's that?"

"You have to text me when you get home. Otherwise I'll worry myself into a tizzy." He flashed that infectious smile again.

"A tizzy, huh?" Mary smiled back. They took out their phones and traded contact info. She lifted a leg over the bike frame, preparing to leave. It was a little taller than she would have liked, but Mary was sure she could manage.

"Hey, Mary," Griff said, grabbing onto the handlebars. "He's going to be okay."

Mary tightened her lips, wishing she could believe it. "Thank you. I mean it. You came along at the perfect time. And you were . . . really kind." Maybe because she felt vulnerable and off-balance, Mary felt an impulse to lean in and give Griff a quick peck on the lips. He had such nice, full lips. It would have been such a bold move, and totally unlike her, but that was how she felt in that moment. There was something going on between them.

It was exciting, pedaling home, to think about something positive for a change. In this case, a very not-bad-looking boy who could be extremely sweet when he wanted to be.

12

[excluded]

"THEY'RE HERE, I'M LEAVING FOR THE BEACH NOW!" Mary shouted upstairs. She waited a beat, heard no reply. No surprise. It was an uneasy feeling, though, this acute awareness that her mother wasn't paying attention. Mary didn't know what to do about it, if anything. Maybe it was a good thing. Part of growing up. Freedom, not neglect. Besides, her mom could always text later if she needed details.

Mary climbed into the backseat of Mrs. Brown's blue Lexus. Chrissie slid over to make room. The air inside was immediately cool. Alexis sat in the front passenger seat. "Mom, you've met Mary, remember?"

Mrs. Brown turned to flash Mary a bright smile. "Of course, the birthday party, am I right?"

"Yep, that's me! I was the one who ate six red velvet cupcakes, I think," Mary joked. "I love your sunglasses, Mrs. Brown. Very fashion forward!" And it was true. Mary truly did like Mrs. Brown's sleek, dark sunglasses. Mrs. Brown had one of those faces Mary saw in magazines: sharp cheekbones, flawless skin, perfect nose—even a football helmet would have looked stylish on that head. Mary prided herself on good manners with parents. Complimenting Mrs. Brown's sunglasses was simply part of Mary's "manners-plus" policy.

"Hi, Chrissie. I love that top. It matches your eyes," Mary said. That was another thing good friends do. They compliment each other. "Are we picking up Chantel?" Mary asked.

Chrissie glanced at Alexis. "No, I don't think so."

"Not today!" Alexis chirped, eyes twinkling with mischief.

Chrissie snickered.

Mary could tell there was something swimming beneath the surface. A shark in these waters. She glanced at Mrs. Brown, who didn't seem to be listening. "Did something happen?"

"Let's just say, she's not included anymore," Alexis said. "We'll leave it at that."

Chrissie nodded in agreement.

"But—" Mary began.

"No one is telling you what to do, Mary," Chrissie said. There was something rough in her tone, though for dissonance she placed a warm hand on Mary's forearm. "You can be friends with whomever you want. It's just . . . Alexis and I are not happy with Chantel. So whatever. We can talk about it later." The way Chrissie leaned into those words—you can be friends with whomever you want—caused Mary's heartbeat to accelerate. There was something going on. Mary didn't want their summer friendship to slip away.

For the rest of the ride, zipping down Wantagh Parkway to Jones Beach, Mary played with her seat's individual climate-zone controls and pondered the Chantel situation. Could a person be in at one moment, and then out the very next? It sure seemed like it. Mary wondered what Chantel had done wrong. It must have been pretty bad.

Mrs. Brown pulled into the Field Four parking lot. It was clear that she was one of those highly organized Beach Moms. She popped the trunk and out came a cart with two fat wheels, filled with towels and brightly colored bags and beach chairs. "Grab that cooler, will you, Lexi?" Mrs. Brown instructed. It was also on wheels and had a long white handle. Mrs. Brown tilted her flawless head and let the sun smile down upon her like an old friend. "Every day at the beach is a good day," she purred, slinging a large beach bag over her shoulder. "Let's see: sunscreen, book, cooler, blankets, purse, phone. I think we're good to go, girls. What do you say? Let's beat the rush."

There were lots of different types of mothers in the world, and their children were basically stuck with what they got. Which was perfectly fine. It's not like Mary looked around and thought, *I'd like to trade in mine for that one*. Mrs. Brown was a classic Long Island sun worshipper. In other words, totally different from Mary's mother, who sunburned easily and thus walked around with globs of zinc oxide on her nose—indoors!

Alexis sidled up to Mary and whispered, "Don't worry, we'll ditch my mother once we get there. She reads for a while, has a plastic glass of wine, then she lays out for serious tanning. We can hang out on the boardwalk and do whatever we want."

13

[boardwalk]

ONCE THEY ARRIVED AT MRS. BROWN'S USUAL SPOT, not far from the lifeguard stand, they stripped down to their bathing suits (even Mrs. Brown, who looked yoga-toned in a lime green bikini). Mary gazed toward the ocean. The waves rolled in shapely, tight curls. A little big, but not too scary. "Want to swim?" she asked.

"Maybe later," Alexis said. "Do you have any money, Mom? We're feeling snackish. And we might wanna play putt-putt."

Mrs. Brown absently dug into her bag, snapped open a small purse, and handed her daughter fifty dollars. "I have sliced watermelon, grapes, drinks, and health bars in the cooler, so don't buy too much junk." Mary felt a warm flash of embarrassment rise to her cheeks.

"Sure, Mom," Alexis said. In a flash, the girls were weaving through the beach blankets that covered the white sand, crowded with bodies of every shape and size. Hairy men with bursting bellies who looked like they'd swallowed basketballs, beefy frat boys with red plastic cups, young families who set up little pup tents to keep their toddlers safe in the shade. The three girls eagerly strode up to the boardwalk, which ran two miles from end to end and had concessions and freshwater pools alongside tennis and basketball courts. The sun sizzled and the place was packed. On a summer Sunday on Long Island, Jones Beach was a glorious place to be.

After purchasing soft drinks and a bountiful supply of candy—Nerds, Sour Patch Kids, shoelace licorice, and some rapidly melting taffy—the girls found an unoccupied bench that looked out over the famous white sand beach. Seagulls wheeled overhead, ready to scavenge fallen french fries and hot dogs and pizza crusts or whatever other litter they could devour.

The girls divided up the loot and chewed thoughtfully. "Did you really want to play putt-putt?" Mary asked. "I didn't bring a lot of money, but I'm happy to watch."

Chrissie waved a hand. "Oh, Alexis always says that to get more money. We never play."

"But if my mom asks," Alexis said, smiling, "you have to lie!"

"As long as I can say that I won," Mary replied, and the three of them laughed. The beach, the sun, the lifeguards, and the sea. Three friends with the whole day in front of them. You couldn't beat it. Like the T-shirts said, LIFE IS GOOD.

Chrissie gave Alexis a look. She turned to Mary, "So we heard you've been with Griffin Connelly."

"With Griff?" Mary echoed. She was shocked. They had heard? "One time, we had ice cream together. How did you know?"

Chrissie grinned. "We know everyone, Mary. Small town, people talk. There are no secrets."

"So?" Alexis said. "Tell us. What's been going on with you two?"

"Nothing, jeez," Mary said.

Chrissie laughed. "Now, now. We're all friends

here." She made an X across her chest. "We won't say anything."

Mary felt a flush of embarrassment on her cheeks.

"We ran into each other, that's all," she said. Mary thought back about that night, how upset she had been about Jonny, and how Griffin had been so nice. It wasn't something she wanted to share with Alexis or Chrissie or anyone. They were great friends, but not for sharing stuff like that. Besides, there was nothing, really, to share.

"No texting?" Chrissie prodded.

"A little," Mary admitted.

"Flirty pictures?"

"Gross! No!" Mary squealed.

"Ooooh!" Alexis teased. "A little texting, huh? Mary O'Malley and Griffin Connelly, very interesting. I didn't see that coming."

"Come on, it's not anything," Mary countered, a little annoyed with their teasing. But it left Mary wondering if maybe she had missed something important. If maybe their meeting was bigger than she'd realized? Was it a date? What was a date anyway? "I borrowed his bike. So we had to coordinate."

"Mm-hmmm," Chrissie said.

"Uh-huh," Alexis cooed.

"Strictly professional," Mary said, slashing the air with a flat hand.

"Well, since we're talking boys," Alexis confided, "I've decided I'm interested in Hakeem." She allowed her gaze to linger on Mary for an extra moment. It was as if she had pointed out a cute pair of shoes in a shop window. The next day, or soon after, you knew they'd be on her feet.

Hakeem. That is surprising, thought Mary. And in her mind, two dots connected. The trouble with Chantel. And now this. "Does he like you?" Mary asked.

Chrissie laughed. "Ha! I'm sure he does—Hakeem just doesn't know it yet!" She acted as if this was hilarious, the funniest thing anyone could have possibly said.

"Stop," Alexis said, but she was laughing, too.

Mary's phone buzzed. A text from Chantel, explaining that she was going away to camp for two weeks. She wanted to say goodbye. Mary ignored it. Chantel would figure it out soon enough.

She'd been unfriended.

14

[missing]

AND SO THE LAST WEEKS OF SUMMER ROLLED ALONG.
Mary's way of dealing with discord was to stay away
from home as much as possible. She thought of the
turmoil of her house as a garbage disposal. You didn't
want to stick your hand in there. Keep busy, keep doing
stuff, that was the strategy. When Mary had to be home,
she lingered in her room or blobbed in front of the TV,
passing a bowl of pretzels back and forth with Ernesto.
He was a nuggets man, and Mary approved. Mary
felt relaxed only when she hung out with Alexis and
Chrissie. She didn't have to think about things. Lately
Tamara Agee had joined them. She was a perfectly nice

girl who functioned as Chantel's replacement. Together they served as the easygoing distraction that kept Mary from remembering how bone-deep miserable she really felt. She laughed, thinking, *It's like eating marshmallows*.

After a trip to the mall on Wednesday with Chrissie—it was just the two of them, not a triangle or a rectangle but a straight line!—Mary paused on her modest front stoop. It was always like that now. Take a deep breath. Back straight, shoulders squared. She pushed open the door, eased into the silent house. Her mother looked up expectantly. She sat in the living room on a cushioned bench tucked beside the bay window that looked out over the front yard. Mary's mother leaned forward, knees together, a phone cradled in her hands. Mary saw the spasm of disappointment on her face.

"Hoping for someone else?" Mary said.

"Jonny's been gone for two days without a word," Mrs. O'Malley said. Her face was drawn, with gravity and stress pulling it down.

"HE'S BEEN GONE ALMOST FORTY-EIGHT HOURS."

Mary sank into a chair across from her mother, waited.

Mrs. O'Malley continued, "I've called all the hospitals, the police. I've checked with his old friends. Nobody knows where he is." She looked out the large front window, as if willing her son to skip up the path. There was nothing, no one.

"You look tired, Mom," Mary said. "Have you eaten?"

Mrs. O'Malley wasn't listening. She swiped at her phone with a forefinger, stared down, frowned. "He hasn't posted anything on social media," she said, not bothering to look up. As if she were alone in the world, talking to herself. "It's like he's vanished."

"He's probably all right," Mary said. "He's done this before."

Mrs. O'Malley nodded, sucked on her lower lip.

"You can't keep doing this to yourself, Mom," Mary said.

After a pause, Mrs. O'Malley looked up. Confusion swam in her eyes. "What? Did you say—?"

"I'll make you tea," Mary said, rising. "What kind would you like?"

"You decide."

"Mom?"

No reply. Mary stood, annoyed. "Mom!" she repeated in a sharper voice.

Her mother looked up from the phone, startled. Her eyes shimmered, like wet stones in a riverbed. "I don't know, I don't know what kind of tea. It doesn't matter. None of it matters," she said. And her hands reminded Mary of nervous birds, plump little wrens hopping about the understory, pecking away for seeds and bugs. Her mother didn't know what to do with her hands.

"I'll make Raspberry Zinger with honey," Mary decided. "Do we have cookies? Never mind. I'll look."

In the kitchen, Mary waited for the water to boil. She texted Griffin: *Hey, favor. We're trying to locate my brother. Do you think maybe one of your sisters might know? The one who lives in town? I forget her name. Could you check?*

No signs of dinner tonight. It was almost six. Ernesto didn't seem to be around; his orange pickup truck wasn't in the driveway. *So mac and cheese again*, Mary thought. There are worse things.

A moment later, Griff texted. *Sure. Vivvy. I'll let you know.*

And seconds after that, another one followed: *You okay?*

The teapot whistled.

Mary stared at the screen, not knowing how to answer. Was she okay? *Not great, no*, she finally replied, then pocketed the phone.

It was nice of Griff to ask. More than what she was getting from anyone at home. Mary piled four Triple Berry Fig Newtons on a plate—a massively underrated cookie, in Mary's opinion—and brought two cups of tea into the living room.

"We went to the mall," Mary informed her mother. "It was fun."

Mrs. O'Malley nodded. Lifted the cup, but neglected to take a sip. "Did you get anything?"

"A T-shirt that says 'Give Peas a Chance' and some funny socks about kale." Mary paused, then added, "I didn't have much money. You said you were going to take me, so . . ."

Mrs. O'Malley brought a hand to her neck, smoothing it. "I did, didn't I?"

"Last week," Mary said.

Her mother seemed to absorb those words. She

slumped under the weight, the downward pull of gravity again.

"It's okay, Mom. There's been a lot going on."

They sat quietly for a while. Tea was a bad call on a hot day, but it seemed to fit her mother's mood. Melancholy and iced tea didn't mix.

"Where's Ernesto?" Mary asked, hoping to generate some non-Jonny conversation. "I haven't seen him lately."

"We're taking a time-out." Mrs. O'Malley looked down, working hard not to betray any emotion. She carefully placed the hot cup on the table. "He needs a break from all this . . . kerfuffle."

The thing with worry and sadness, Mary thought, was how they filled a room. The air became heavy with them; they formed a thick fog that was hard to walk through. When you breathed in, you brought the sadness down deep into your lungs, and when you breathed out, some of the worry got stuck inside. It became part of your body. She cautiously suggested, "You shouldn't let Jonny talk to him like that."

Her mother cringed, as if stung. She studied her fingernails, nodding slightly. "It's been hard for Jonny. He remembers his father."

"Yeah, but."

"I know, you're right, I shouldn't make excuses for him," Mrs. O'Malley said, reading Mary's thoughts. "I keep making the same mistakes."

"And maybe," Mary ventured, "the screaming doesn't work?"

Mary's mother actually laughed out loud. "You think? Ha! Can I just"—she balled her hands into fists—"mash him on the foot with a bowling ball instead?"

It was funny and real. Their first true moment in months. The laughter, for that brief instant, chased the sorrow from Mary's throat.

Her phone dinged. A text from Griff: *Found him*.

15
[staying]

LESS THAN AN HOUR LATER, A CAR PULLED UP IN front of the house. Jonny got out, gave a two-fingered salute goodbye, and a dented green atrocity of a car sped off. Barefoot Jonny swerved up the walkway. He was dressed oddly, wearing clothes Mary didn't recognize: shiny baby blue gym shorts and a ratty green sweatshirt. Not his clothes, Mary decided. I wonder what happened to them? Anyway, a weird combination to wear in August. Mary glanced at her mother. She was clenching and unclenching her fists, staring straight ahead. She blew air out of her mouth in a long, slow, determined exhale.

Trying hard to stay calm.

"Here comes Jonny," Mary whispered, recalling that scene from *The Shining*. It was a bad joke that didn't land. The timing was off. If Mary and her mother had laughed just minutes before, it now felt like a hundred years ago. Jonny stood before them like a diaphanous phantom. He looked light, delicate, and insubstantial, his skin pale to the point of translucent. If it was possible, he seemed dramatically thinner than just two days ago. Had he eaten anything at all? Had he slept? No matter how bright and shiny the drugs made him feel, this was how he looked when he crashed from that euphoric high. There were scratch marks on his right cheek, near his eye.

"Oh, Jonny," his mother gasped. "I've been worried sick."

He ran a hand through his unkempt hair. "I can explain."

"Please."

Jonny's eyes cast about. He seemed unsure whether he should stand or sit or collapse on the floor. "I lost my phone."

"You lost—?"

"I knew you'd flip out," Jonny snapped. "That's

so typical!" He flailed an arm, a wild gesture that nearly pulled him off-balance.

Mrs. O'Malley closed her eyes, paused, opened them again. "I will try," she said, her voice cold but steady, "to not flip out. I apologize. Where is your phone?"

"I lost it," Jonny said. "So how would I know where it is? That's a ridiculous question."

Mary interrupted. "Do you want some water? Or juice?"

Jonny looked at her and nodded. "Juice. Thanks, May."

Mary got up, poured a tall glass of orange juice, and brought it to Jonny. He sat hunched over, elbows on his knees, facing his mother. He took a long drink of juice, and Mary could hear the *glug, glug, glug* as it went down his parched gullet.

"I didn't know where you were."

"I couldn't call. I lost my phone," Jonny insisted.

Mrs. O'Malley shook her head. "You could have borrowed a phone. You could have—"

"I didn't remember your number," he countered. "No one remembers numbers anymore, Mom."

"I called the police. Every hospital. Your friends from school . . ."

"Mom! What is the big deal? I lost my phone. Okay, yeah, granted, that sucks. I'll get a new one. I'm nineteen years old. I lived away at college, remember? I'm used to having my freedom—"

"I thought you were dead," Mary's mother said. Her lips trembled and her voice cracked at the end, that last word splitting in two. Everyone in the room, including Jonny, rocked by the wake of that utterance. Even he had to hear the raw pain and heartbreak of that stark declaration.

I thought you were dead.

"I—" Jonny stopped himself, his hands traveling to his temples. "I'm sorry. I'm so, so, so sorry, Mom."

He tried a new tact. "The truth is . . . I was afraid to call. I knew you'd be angry."

"Wait, no," Mary's mother said. Her voice took on a sharper edge, the decibels rising. "This is my fault? You didn't call and it is my fault?"

"Mom," Mary said softly.

Mrs. O'Malley glared for a moment, then nodded. "Mary, I'm not sure you should be here right now. Please give your brother and me some time alone. This is a private conversation between Jonny and myself."

"I don't agree," Mary replied. She made no move to leave. "This is my family, too. I'm not leaving."

16
[choices]

"I KNOW I MAKE YOU MISERABLE," JONNY SAID, SHIFT-
ing strategies once again. "I know you hate me, Mom.
I don't blame you. Just let me go."

"I don't hate you. Don't ever say that," his mother
shot back. "I hate what these drugs are doing to you.
I hate it, I hate it, I hate it. But I will never let you go,
so forget that. Not an option."

She opened a drawer from the coffee table and
pulled out a handful of objects: a ball of aluminum
foil, a plastic medicine bottle half-filled with blue
pills, a lighter, a pipe, a spoon, a baggie of weed. "I
found this in your room," Mrs. O'Malley said. Her

hand trembled slightly as she held it out like an offering. "This is yours, right? This is what you bring into our home?"

Jonny didn't flinch. He just shook his head. "You went searching around in my room?"

"Don't, don't even," his mother warned.

Then she surprised both of her children. Mary watched as Mrs. O'Malley took a deep breath, sat up tall, back erect, and calmly dropped the items to the floor. Somehow she had transformed before their eyes. She spoke in a slow, clear voice that surely required her every ounce of self-control. "I've learned some things over these past two and a half years," she began. "Slowly, painfully. Mistake after mistake. And number one: I can't do anything for you, except love you.

"I've tried yelling, and threatening, and spying—and I see now that it hasn't worked. You need to make your own choices, Jonny, for your own reasons. You often remind me that you are nineteen years old. That's true. Legally, I can't force you to do anything, and," she raised a hand, "I would not, even if I could, because I no longer believe it would help in the long run. Change has to come from you. I've been wrong and I'm sorry. I am so sorry for my failures and my mistakes. But now you have to move out. You can't live in this house any longer."

"Mom," Jonny began.

"I'm not finished," she stated, cutting him off. "I've learned that all my worrying hasn't helped you. It's only hurt. It's hurt this family, it's hurt your sister, it's hurt my relationships, and it's hurt me."

She rose to her feet, smiled tightly. "I do not approve of the choices you make. I will help you if you sincerely seek help: a program, a therapist, inpatient, outpatient, medication, whatever it takes. If you want to walk that road, if you are ready, I will walk by your side."

For a moment, Mary could see her mother almost lose it. She looked down, blinked back the tears, her entire body trembling with emotion, and then miraculously pulled herself together again. All Mary could think during those painful, awful moments, was this:

Go, Mom.

"I hope you will come to see that you are harming yourself," she said. "But what you choose with your life is up to you. I will do nothing that contributes to your substance use disorder. I won't cook you dinner,

I won't do your laundry, I won't pay your rent. You must listen to me, Jonny. Because listening to yourself is not working. Nothing changes if nothing changes. If you stay on this path, you will die."

Jonny absorbed every word, pale and subdued. He looked exhausted. Mrs. O'Malley picked up her cup and saucer. She walked out of the room in an act that took courage and supreme concentration. And she was gone, leaving behind only an echo. Mary heard her mother's footsteps stop in the hallway, then turn around and march back. Standing at the archway, she pointed a shaking finger at her son. "To be clear, Jonny, so there is no mistaking this conversation. I want you out of this house. You will find a place. You will get a job. Yes, I will help you make this transition. But that's where it stops. The rest is up to you. By the end of the month, I want you gone, or I will personally throw all your things out into the street for all the neighborhood to see."

17

[griff]

GRIFF ROLLED UP TO MARY'S HOUSE ON A SILVER, fat-wheeled bike. Mary knew he was coming and waited out front with his borrowed bike leaning against a tree.

Mary gestured to the bike, "I thought you were coming to pick up—"

"Nah, you keep it. I've got this one now." Griff stepped off his bike and carelessly let it drop to the ground. "You cut your hair."

It was true. Mary had cut her hair. Just grabbed a pair of scissors and did it herself last night. She didn't have complicated hair, long and straight, and now it wasn't as long—by about six uneven inches. It barely reached her shoulders. "Is it okay?" she asked. "I just felt like doing it."

"Wait, you cut it yourself?" Amusement played in Griff's voice. He mimed frantically snipping at his own hair.

"So?"

"It's awesome—good for you. It's cool to have the confidence to, you know," Griff paused, smiling, "not care if your head looks like a mangled bush."

"Yeah, I used garden shears," Mary quipped. "Is it really bad?"

"You look great," Griff replied. And the way he said it, there was something there, as if he'd accidentally stumbled into a genuine compliment. He raised his chin, gestured to the house. "How's your brother? All good?"

"Sleeping," Mary said.

They had texted during the previous night, puzzling together a rough outline of Jonny's whereabouts. It all centered around him hanging out with Vivvy, Griff's sister, along with a bunch of their friends at her downtown apartment. Generally speaking, Mary wasn't eager to share the family secrets—

substance use, addiction, a brother thrown out of the house—with friends and neighbors. That stuff was their family's business, a story they didn't want to tell. Still, it felt good to have someone to confide in, someone who understood, someone she could trust.

"Do you think they're a thing?" Mary asked. "My brother and Vivvy? That's so weird."

"I doubt they define themselves that way," Griff said, shrugging innocently. "What's weird about it?"

Mary blushed, didn't answer. It was obvious what was weird about it. Griff seemed to enjoy making Mary uncomfortable.

"Come on, let's go," Griff said. "And don't tell me you don't have a bicycle, because I know you do."

Mary looked back at the house. She should tell someone. "Where do you want to go?"

"I thought we'd ride around until we find trouble. Old Mill Pond? There's a decent bike trail that loops around. Go to a deli, grab subs. I have money. That okay with you?"

They pedaled for twenty minutes, Griffin weaving and chattering and performing minor stunts. Mary enjoyed the ache in her quads, working the pedals, keeping up, the physical freedom of the breeze in her face. Once they arrived at the pond, they pulled off under a great old oak. There weren't many people around. Griff got up to harass some geese, chasing them around, arms flailing like wings.

"Griff, don't," Mary said. "You're scaring them."

Griff widened his eyes, hands on his chest. "*Moi?* Seriously? These geese are nasty. Look at the ground, there's mounds of green poop everywhere. Besides, *they will attack*. I'm actually risking my life here."

But rather than prolong bickering about the wildlife, Griff plopped down beside Mary on the grass.

"I don't understand why he won't stop," Mary said. "I miss him but can't stand to be near him. I love him, but I don't like him. Maybe it's good he moves out."

Griff looked at her, tossed a stone into the water. "You need to start thinking about other things," he said. "It can't be Jonny-Jonny all the time."

Mary knew he was right.

But it annoyed her just the same.

18
[favor]

A WEEK LATER, JONNY WAS READY TO MOVE OUT. AN older guy Jonny knew, Dez Ramirez, had a place in town and for some reason was glad to take Jonny in—provided he paid the first two months' rent in advance. Maybe Dez wasn't a dummy after all. Once the plan was decided, the mood in the house lifted. Jonny wasn't as sour anymore. He was almost giddy. He ate meals, slept, slowly returned to something approximating his former self. Even better, Mary's mother didn't seem as jangled and distracted. She accepted the new reality. At peace with it for now. Ernesto showed up one day after work with a friend, sweating and grunting and hauling a used NordicTrack Elliptical Trainer up the stairs and into the master bedroom. Ernesto bought it off Craigslist and decorated it with a big yellow ribbon and bow.

"Some gift, he just wants me to get back in shape," Mrs. O'Malley joked, but Mary could tell that she was happy and touched by the gesture.

"It needs a little work," Ernesto admitted, winking at Mary, "but don't we all?"

Miracle of miracles, Jonny landed a job at a bagel shop in town—"They have the single best garlic bagels on the planet!" he enthused—so it felt like things were moving in the right direction. Summer was winding down, school was starting in less than two weeks. Sure, there was still a lot to worry about. Would Jonny actually go to work? Could he feed himself? Would he slide back into more partying, more drugs, more dangerous decisions? No one knew the answers to those questions. Not even Jonny.

ON THE DAY BEFORE HER BROTHER MOVED OUT, MARY sat in the backyard at a reclaimed picnic table that Ernesto had "rescued" from someone's garbage pile.

He did that a lot. Drove around in his pickup truck on garbage day, often returning with curbside items of questionable quality. A riding lawn mower that "only" needed a new fuel pump and starter switch; a boat that leaked; a set of ancient, rusted golf clubs; a battered ping pong table that lacked a net. *He has a weakness for broken things,* Mary mused. The thought sank down into her belly, like a small stone dropped into a well, and it made her appreciate Ernesto just a little more.

Mary set out her art supplies. Paper, brushes, watercolors. She painted a seated female figure, facing away, balancing a stack of rocks on her head. It was a strange, almost magical image and it pleased Mary to make it. An hour passed. Very quietly, Jonny sat down beside her. He wore pajama bottoms and a T-shirt. His hair was wet from the shower. Mary didn't comment, but she felt surprised. He didn't usually show much interest. Why was he here?

"That's pretty good," Jonny said. "I like it."

Mary grunted softly.

"Do you mind if I—?"

Mary tilted her head, glanced sideways. She tore out a thick sheet of paper from her spiral-bound sketch pad, slid it over. Jonny picked up a spare brush, dipped it in water, and looked around the yard, seeking inspiration.

"No paintings of me, please," Mary said. "I'm still scarred from that drawing you did when I was in first grade. I looked like an anteater!"

Jonny laughed, a full-throated hoot. It was a sound Mary hadn't heard in a while. It hung in the air, floated amid the trees, and drifted up to the clouds. Something as simple as a laugh. Mary wished she could paint it. Jonny's laughter. She missed it.

They worked in silence, shoulder to shoulder. Then Jonny said, "I'm moving out tomorrow, you know."

Mary rocked with her body, a sort of nod.

"It'll be good," he said. "I'm super psyched."

Mary didn't answer. Just listened, hunched over her painting, mixing the blues.

"Mom seems cool about it," he ventured. "Like maybe it's best."

"Uh-huh," Mary commented.

Jonny leaned back, studying her. He raised a thumb, squinting like an artist before an easel. "You got your hair cut."

"Last week," Mary said.

"I know, I know!" Jonny smiled. He hadn't noticed. It only dawned on him now, when he was suddenly making this awkward attempt to be friendly.

A *show* of friendliness.

A performance.

Compliments and smiles.

Mary wondered if it was a real smile or an imitation of one.

"Remember that time you got bubblegum in your hair?" Jonny asked.

"I slept on it," she recalled. "It must have fallen out of my mouth. I was crying."

"I tried to cut it out for you," Jonny recalled, laughing. "That was a bad idea! Your head came out looking lopsided!"

Mary remembered. Because she was the kind of person who remembered everything. All the good times and the bad. Jonny had lost interest in his painting of the tree. The browns and greens had gotten muddy. It wasn't very good. He flicked the brush like a dart into the water glass. A splash and a clink.

"So, um," he began.

Mary turned to look directly at him. She placed

the palms of both hands on the table as if steadying herself, a gesture that unconsciously imitated her mother. Mary knew what this was. She knew her brother. So she waited for it to come.

His knee was bobbing up and down again. He was high. Mary was sure of it. Something about the way his gaze couldn't quite settle on any object, like a butterfly that refused to land. "I feel like a jerk asking. Especially my little sister. Dez and I really want to fix the place up. Get a rug for the living room, a microwave, you know, make it really sharp, like a home."

Mary nodded as if she believed every word.

"But I'm just kind of hurting for money right now," Jonny said. "It's totally temporary. I'm going to pay you back. I'm scheduled for a ton of hours at Gateway Bagels, I'll be working all the time, so I'm totally good for it, but I won't get paid for, like, at least, I don't know, two weeks . . ."

"What about Mom? I thought she gave you money."

Jonny rolled his eyes. "Yeah, barely. For rent. She's not even giving me money for food. She insists on taking me grocery shopping. Like I'm a baby."

"She doesn't trust you," Mary said.

Jonny opened his mouth, ready to argue. Desperation flickered in his eyes. He looked away, picked at the table with his fingernail, peeling off a splinter of wood. "Look, I know. It hasn't been good. I screwed up. A lot. But I'm changing, Mary. This is my chance to start over."

"I don't have much," Mary said.

"What about that birthday money from Grams?" Jonny ventured. There was urgency in his voice, new hope. "She gave you, like, two hundred dollars, right? Do you still have that?"

Mary was saving that money. She wanted to buy some things for herself. Maybe a denim jacket. More art supplies. More things.

Just things.

"Okay," she relented. "But I need it back, every cent."

Jonny's eyes lit up. A smile wriggled across his face like a snake moving through the grass. "Oh man, that's so awesome. Thank you, Mary, thank you, thanks a million," he gushed. "I'll pay you back, I promise."

"Sure," she said. "I believe you."

Because, really, what else was there to say?

19
[bikes]

GRIFFIN, CODY, AND MARY RACED THEIR BIKES ALONG a network of dirt trails in the woods behind the middle school. Even under the relative cool of the shaded canopy, they dripped with sweat from their exertion. It was a scorching day, and not even noon yet. Over the years different bikers had built up hills and ramps, working on their own with shovels and muscle, to create a private paradise.

"I never knew this place existed," Mary marveled, guzzling from her water bottle.

Cody was preparing to perform a dangerous stunt.

Griff cupped his hands around his mouth, cheering him on. "All right, Cody! Go big or go home!"

Cody paused at the top of a medium incline, which led down to two ramps. A small one, which most everybody used, and a much larger one, reserved for maniacs and reckless daredevils. Cody pushed off on his right leg, rose up on both pedals, and fearlessly bombed down the hill at max speed. He hit the big ramp and flew, handlebars almost vertical over the seat. The back tire bounced heavily on the dirt and skidded; thrown off the bike, Cody rolled and tumbled with a meaty thud. The bike smacked into a thicket of underbrush. Mary stepped forward. "Oh my God."

There was a pause, when every injury seemed possible—cracked ribs, a broken leg, a severed spine—and then Cody raised a hand, thumbs up, and laughed out loud.

"That was sick!" Griff enthused. "Cody, my man, you are a beast!"

Mary had been hanging out more with Griff this past week. Not every day, but regularly, if tentatively. She still wasn't sold on him. He had an edge that was intriguing but also . . . *off* somehow. Still, he was the only person on the planet she could talk to about Jonny, and right now she needed that. Alexis and Chrissie were vacationing together on the Jersey Shore. Chrissie's parents allowed her to invite one friend, once more making the hierarchy of middle school friendship an easy chart to read. It came in the shape of a pyramid—a three-dimensional triangle, known to math whizzes like Mary as a tetrahedron—and she was closer to the base than the apex. It bummed her out a little, to be left out. And with Chantel's status unclear, Mary either kept to herself or joined Griff and his revolving galaxy of knuckleheads on their daily escapades. Mary wasn't sure where she fit with Griff's crowd, or even if she wanted to, but it was better than sitting home alone munching marshmallows and staring at the fish tank.

Speaking of knuckleheads, up rolled one of Mary's least favorite people: Drew Peterson, a hulking, super-sketchy dude who fulfilled every caveman stereotype. Griff seemed to respect Drew for some reason, and in that trying-not-trying way of his, he schemed to earn Drew's admiration.

"Droop," Griff said in greeting.

And more melodically, "Droopy!" from Cody.

"Figured I might find you here," Drew said. He climbed off his bike, holding a white plastic bag. "Man, it's stupid hot! You guys seen Sinjay? I wouldn't mind jumping in his pool."

He gazed open-mouthed at Mary, who sat cross-legged on the ground in her shorts. No hello, just the look. Something about him made her skin crawl. He wasn't the brightest bulb, either. Probably took too many shots to the helmet in Pop Warner football. Good nickname, though. Drew Peterson got shortened to Drew P., then Droopy or just Droop. The group dynamic tilted whenever he came around, and all of a sudden Mary wished she were anywhere else. Mathematically, Griff's kindness to Mary was in inverse proportion to the number of people who were around. The more witnesses, the colder he got. The nice boy from the ice cream parlor was a million miles away. *Where did he go?* Mary wondered.

"Sweet bike," Droopy noted. "New?"

Griff nodded, grinned.

"Dig the shocks," Droopy said.

"Cody installed 'em for me. Changes the look, you know?" Griff said.

"I'd love a bike like that," Droopy gushed. "If you ever see one that needs a home."

Griff glanced at Mary. "I'll keep it in mind."

"Yep, yep," Cody chirped.

Mary found that whole exchange suspicious. What was up with Griff and bicycles? He gave her one. How weird was that? Who gives bikes away?

"Hey, check this," Droopy said. "I found all these ketchup packets behind McDonalds!" He opened the plastic bag to reveal dozens of individual ketchup packets.

"Okaaaaay," Griff said.

"No, it's hysterical. Watch this," Droop said. He placed a packet on a flat rock and stomped on it with his foot. *Splat*, the ketchup squirted an impressive distance.

"Whoa," Cody said, "let me try."

So that's what they did: splattered ketchup on the trees and bushes, leaving plastic wrappers all over the ground. Mary stretched, grumbled, checked her phone. Boredom in the suburbs was a terrible thing. It led to all kinds of idiocy. "I might head out," she said.

The boys went with her, maybe just for something to do, feeling just as restless. They threaded a path behind the middle school to the football field and the track that surrounded it. "Hey, look," Cody said. "There's your buddy, Griff."

He pointed to a lone figure shuffling along the track. He wore a short-sleeved, button-down shirt and long pants. Not exactly the outfit of a track star. Curly hair, pear-shaped body. Mary recognized him as David Hallenback, one of the kids in school she tended to ignore.

Griffin's face brightened. "Hallenback. God, that kid is so annoying. Let's say hello."

"Yep, yep, yep," Cody agreed.

"Oh, this'll be good," Droopy said, still clutching his half-filled plastic bag.

Mary followed along.

20
[ketchup]

MARY DIDN'T HAVE A CLUE WHAT WAS GOING TO HAP-pen next, but she didn't have a good feeling based on the look of disgust on Griffin's face. David Hallenback was a stumpy-legged kid who was not the type who'd be pals with Griffin Connelly. Yet when David looked up to see the four bicyclists pedaling his way, he offered up a worshipful greeting. "Griff! Hey!"

Griffin pedaled swiftly toward David, rising on the pedals, as if he was going to ram straight into him before braking hard at the last second.

David recoiled, then laughed with relief, look-ing around at the group. "Funny, Griff!" Hallenback looked hot and tired. He was dressed in jeans and his shirt had huge sweat stains along the back and under the armpits. His freckled face was flushed and blotchy.

"What are you doing out here, Hallenback? Are you . . . exercising?" Griff asked in a tone of disbelief.

"Yes," David said, raising his fists in a gesture of pumping weights. "I'm in training!"

Droopy snickered.

The boys got off their bikes. Mary, too.

"So explain it to me," Griff said. "I don't understand. You don't strike me as the exercising type."

David chuckled, his small dark eyes shimmering. "My uncle Lewis said he'd give me a fifty dollar gift certificate to any store at the mall if I can run a full mile without stopping."

Griff whistled. "Wow, no stopping, huh? How's it going?"

David grinned impishly. Mary thought he was almost cute, in a basset hound puppy kind of way. "Today, I made it almost once all the way around," he said, not without pride.

"Once!" Griff barked. "You hear that, Mary? One time. What's a mile? Four times?"

"Four times around," Cody said. "Yep, yep, yep."

"Oh," David said, somehow not aware of that basic fact. He pulled at the front of his wet, sticky shirt.

"I wonder if you are sufficiently motivated to run a full mile," Griff mused. "What do you guys think? Is Hallenback trying hard enough?"

"No, he is not," Droopy stated.

David laughed, eagerly looking from face to face, trying to figure out the shift in tone.

Griff grabbed the bag from Droopy's hand. He took out a ketchup packet, tore it open with his teeth. "Here's the new training plan, Hallenback. You start running, right? And if you stop, we squeeze ketchup on you."

The smile on David's face slowly faded.

He tried laughing it off.

"I'm not kidding," Griff said. He patted David on the shoulder. "This is a proven training strategy. We're here to help. This will work, believe me. And then, *ka-ching*, you get fifty bucks. Any store in the mall! You'll be thanking us later."

"Griff," Mary said.

He ignored her.

"You ready, Hallenback? You all limber and everything? Need to do some jumping jacks before you begin?"

"I'm really tired," David said. "It's too hot."

Griffin Connelly reached his hand out over David's head and squeezed out a splatter of ketchup. It dripped onto David's hair.

"Whoa!" Droopy roared, laughing. He clapped his hands.

Hallenback stood in shock, wiping a hand through his hair in disbelief.

"That's not cool, Griff," Mary said.

Griff pulled out another ketchup packet, stared directly at Mary as he tore it open with his teeth. "What are you waiting for, David?" Griffin flashed a wolfish smile. "Do you like being a french fry?"

"He's a french fry, he's a french fry!" Cody sang, bouncing around in amusement.

Droopy reached into the bag, grabbed a handful of packets. "My turn next."

David took one look at Droopy's thuggish face and started to run. The halting, lumbering stride of a nonathlete. He didn't stand a chance. Halfway around the first lap, David began to clutch his side, slowed by a cramp. Griffin and the boys followed him on their bikes, cheering him on.

"Come on, David! You can do it, brother!"

"Think of those fifty dollars!"

"Don't stop, don't you stop," Griff warned.

But of course he did. There was no way on earth David Hallenback could run a full mile in that late August heat. It just wasn't in him. He stopped, bent over, head down, hands on his knees, gasping.

Droopy splattered a packet on his back. Another one on his shoulders.

"He's a french fry!" Cody cried, laughing.

David started jogging again.

Mary grabbed Griffin by the arm. "This is gross. What are you doing? You have to stop it."

"Relax, we're joking around. It's funny," Griff said. His eyes had gone cold. He had switched over to something else, or someone else, darker than Mary had seen before. Droopy watched them argue, amused by it.

"What are you staring at, Droop?" Mary snapped. "Do you always breathe through your mouth?"

Droopy was surprised by her ferocity. Griffin turned to look at him, too, perhaps curious how he'd react to Mary's challenge. Droopy responded by giving a fierce tug on David's shirt, ripping it along the side seam. Forced to the brink, David fought back. He pushed against Droopy, catching the larger boy off-balance. The advantage lasted a second, maybe two. Then, with an explosive two-handed shove, Droopy sent David sprawling to the ground. His head hit with a thud that sounded painful.

"No!" Mary yelled. She stepped beside the fallen boy. "Stop it, or so help me . . ." She pulsed with raw anger, tensed and ready to launch herself at Droopy's throat.

Droopy smirked, unimpressed. "Gee, you're pretty when you're mad. You wanna wrestle?"

"Okay, fun's over," Griff announced with artificial sweetener in his voice. He extended a hand, helping David to his feet. The curly-haired boy, covered in ketchup and shame, stood shaken. Griff smiled. "It's all good now, no worries, Hallenback. Things got a little out of hand. Just kidding around."

David couldn't bring himself to look at the others. He nodded to indicate that he heard the words, but did not, Mary hoped, necessarily agree with the message.

"Droop, apologize to Hallenback."

Droopy stared at Griff for a long moment. "Sorry, Hallenback," he relented.

"Are you hurt?" Griff asked.

David cautiously probed the bump on the back of his head. Checked his fingers for blood.

"All right, you can go home now, Hallenback. Practice is over. You got lucky today. Mary here has a soft heart. She's your guardian angel. But you keep running, Hallenback. Don't you stop," Griff said. "We'll be following you. Go on, get going."

David glanced sideways at Griff. His face remained tilted down and away, the way a beta dog might stand before an alpha. He never glanced toward Mary or the others. Only Griff. "I will," he said, scarcely above a whisper, talking to a spot on the ground. "You'll see. I'll get better." And off he went in his uneven, Hallenback-styled shamble. Bizarrely determined to do his best, as if that were the lesson of the day. To try harder. Not that these guys were cruel and to be avoided at all costs. Not that he had a right to be treated with decency and respect. But that he needed to get better—then his problems might go away. David cut around the school and behind the back. The gang of four—Griff, Cody, Droopy, and Mary—watched him go.

"What a chimp," Droopy said.

"You're an idiot," Mary replied.

"Speaking of french fries," Cody said. "I'm hungry."

21
[court]

NOW IT WAS OUT IN THE OPEN, THE FACT LAID BARE: Mary had witnessed firsthand the cruelty of Griffin Connelly. There was no going back. No thought of friendship or more advanced relationships. All that was over. But Mary couldn't leave the group this minute, not with Hallenback still out there. If she wasn't around, things could get uglier.

"LET'S FOLLOW HIM," GRIFF SAID.

"Hold on," Mary countered, stalling for time. She tried to keep the distress out of her voice, didn't want to sound weak. "Leave him alone. He's not worth it, Griff. We can go swimming or get a slice in town."

Griff looked at her with scorn. "Oh, are you still here, Mary? I thought you had to go home?"

Droopy snickered. He took pleasure in their hostilities.

Mary glared back. "I'm still here."

Griff eyed her for a long pause, then said, "Because if you want to go, then go. Feel free. Nobody's stopping you."

"I know that," she said, staring right back.

Mary gripped the handlebars of the bicycle. Her knuckles went white. She hated being in this position. The way Griff took charge of everyone but somehow made it all seem like it was their choice. The way he cheered on Cody to perform that dangerous stunt— just because Griff thought it would be amusing to watch.

The group pedaled aimlessly on the grass field behind the school. Cody and Droopy chatted and laughed, loose and relaxed; neither Mary nor Griffin spoke a word. There was no sign of Hallenback, but they spotted a boy shooting baskets by himself on the playground court in the distance. Red shorts and a sleeveless tee. Dribble, dribble, dribble—like the sound of a steady heartbeat—then spin, shoot, nothing but net. He was smooth. It made Mary think of Chantel, and a pinprick of regret punctured her heart. Griffin set sail in that direction.

If the boy saw the riders coming, and he must have, he did a good job of not showing it. He set up at the foul line, eyes fixed on the rim, as if nothing else in the world existed but that orange basket. Griff pulled up halfway between the basket and the foul line, directly in the boy's vision. Griff sat balanced on one leg. He crossed his arms, cool as a breeze. Mary fell in with Cody and Droopy, who kept pedaling their bikes, slowly circling like a pack of wolves around vulnerable prey.

"You didn't see anybody come by here, did you?" Griff asked.

"Looks like a french fry," Cody chirped.

The boy had a sweet face, blond hair and long, lanky arms. He looked at Griffin and the others. "I've been shooting around," he shrugged, lifting his chin to indicate the net.

Hmmm, interesting. Mary knew he was lying. And if she knew, it was certain that Griff knew, too.

But how would Griff react? He was unpredictable to her now. What she thought she knew was no longer true. Mary wasn't sure what he'd do next, like an unknown chemical the teacher provided for experiments in science lab. A volatile mixture. Griff slid off his bike and dropped it to the ground like he'd forgotten gravity existed. He clapped his hands, made a target. "Let's see that ball."

The blond boy snapped off a crisp bounce pass. Cody and Droopy dismounted, eager to join this new game. Mary remained seated on her bike, parked to the side, silently watching. The kid looked uncomfortable, but at the same time, he worked hard not to show it. "You new around here?" Griff asked. He took an awkward shot. The ball clanged away.

The kid's name was Eric, they learned. And yes, he was new to the area. Same grade as them.

"When's school start anyway?" Cody asked.

"Thursday the fifth," Mary said. "Twelve days from now."

"At least it's a Thursday," Cody said. "I can handle a two-day week. It should always be that way."

Droopy thought that was a genius idea.

Griff peppered the boy with a series of questions,

half teasing and half curious, testing him. Droopy and Cody bounced around, carrying on a dopey conversation. Just when Mary began to relax, Griff held the ball in his hands. "You don't mind if I keep it for a while, do you?"

It was a clear challenge.

The boy stood motionless, seriously outnumbered. He glanced at Mary, his eyes full of calculation. He was doing the math, Mary decided. And he was gorgeous.

To his credit, Eric played it as cool as he could under the circumstances. He ignored whatever threat floated in the air and pretended everyone was a gang of old pals, hanging out, having a laugh. "I've got to go home in a few minutes—" he began.

Griff bounced the ball back with a one-handed fling. "We're just busting on you," he claimed. It was Griff's way. Friendly one minute, threatening the next, and laughing a moment later, all so no one knew exactly where they stood. There was no clear, firm ground. Griff enjoyed playing with people, like a puppeteer pulling on strings, to see how they reacted under pressure.

Mary feared for this boy. It had already been a bad day, and Droopy added a thuggish element.

"Come on, Griff, let's go. I'm bored," Mary urged.

Griff looked at her, nodded once, as if she had made the most reasonable suggestion he'd heard all week. Leaving was a great idea. But he didn't move a muscle. "So," he said, in that casual manner of his. Just letting the word hang there like a birthday piñata before finally pressing the question, "You really didn't see a kid come through here? For sure?"

The boy blinked. He knew that Griff knew. "I'm just shooting around. I'm like in my own little world out here."

Griff replied that he'd take Eric's word for it—in a way that implied he wasn't buying it. The lie was a painting in a museum and they all kind of stood around, looking at it. For some unknown reason, this new kid was willing to lie to protect David Hallenback, a stranger he didn't know.

Interesting, Mary thought. A hero in red basketball shorts.

The boy tried to salvage the situation. He reasoned, "I mean, I think I would have noticed somebody if—"

"I gotcha," Griffin shot back. "Loud and clear."

They talked some more, Griff mostly full of sarcasm, lies. "We're just looking for one of our buddies, that's all. You can understand that, can't you?" Griff snapped his fingers. An idea popped into his head. He proposed a simple wager: the boy had to take one foul shot from the line. If he hit the shot, he would be allowed to keep his own basketball.

Cody and Droopy perked up, giddy and volatile.

"This is so lame," Mary groaned. She didn't want to see what would happen if the boy missed.

"What do I get if I make it?" the boy asked.

"Ho-ho!" Griff laughed. "Now you're bargaining, huh?"

Having no choice, Eric agreed to the bet.

"I bet a dollar he makes it," Mary volunteered. Eric looked at her. Didn't smile or nod, just blankly looked at the girl on the bike. Mary knew what he saw: she was one of them. It didn't make her feel good.

"You like the looks of him, Mary?" Griff guessed. "The new boy in town?"

Griff knew. He always knew. He had an x-ray gaze for seeing inside people, for knowing what they felt and thought. It was uncanny and very creepy.

Mary didn't like the feeling of exposure it gave her. It was like he could look right through her.

"Let's just get this over with, Griff," she said.

Eric tossed up an air ball, a total choke, and lost the bet. He closed his eyes, shook his head a little, angry at himself or maybe just too stressed to shoot straight.

"Air ball!" chortled Drew P.

Griffin set the ball on the ground, resting his foot on it, and let time slowly pass. Then he gently rolled the ball back to Eric.

"I'm disappointed in you, Eric," Griff commented. "I really thought you'd make that shot." Griff grinned and lifted his bike off the ground. "We'll see you in school. Who knows? Maybe we'll have a few classes together. Wouldn't that be special?" Griff grinned and pedaled away with the others falling in line. They left the boy alone on the court, dazed and confused but unharmed.

"Wait here," Griff told them, and made a U-turn back to the basketball court. Mary and the others watched from fifty yards away. Griff and Eric seemed to talk in a friendly way, a movie on mute. They exchanged smiles and tapped fists. Griff returned.

"What did you say?" Mary asked.

"I told him that I was a good guy to be friends with," Griff said, "and a lousy enemy." He laughed. Cody and Droopy joined in. "I also told him that you think he's cute. Isn't that right, Mary? I saw you looking at him, panting like a dog."

Griff didn't wait for a reaction. He zoomed up ahead, leaving them to follow, knowing they would.

22

[tennis]

THE TEXT FROM CHANTEL HAD COME OUT OF THE blue: *I'm back from camp! Missed you. Let's get together soon! Free Monday?*

Mary hadn't even remembered that Chantel was away at camp. Out of sight, out of mind. But after thinking about it, the fuzzy details emerged from her memory. Chantel went away for two weeks to some progressive camp somewhere in the Berkshires. Activities galore and killer mosquitoes and no phones, no internet. Mary had never been to a sleepaway camp herself, so she had a hard time imagining what one was actually like. Most of what she knew came from random comments from friends or things she'd seen in movies. To her the idea of camp was a mixture of cool things (cabins, a lake) and vaguely horrifying things (icky campers, too much singing, peppy counselors, and forced good cheer).

That explained Chantel's silence. She hadn't just conveniently disappeared. And now Chantel was back again, which was definitely going to be awkward. Meanwhile, Chrissie and Alexis were still vacationing together, probably best-friending themselves into a dither, forgetting all about Mary, the unnecessary third wheel, who was stuck at home during the dog days of late summer.

Jonny had moved out. It changed the house. Not back to normal, exactly, but it no longer felt like there was a bomb about to go off at any second. So that was good, the no-bomb feeling. Still, Mary found herself wondering about her brother, hoping he was okay, and happy, and staying clean, without knowing the answer to any of those things. One positive outcome was that he hadn't lied about the bagels. They were truly awesome. As an act of espionage, Mary's mother swung by Gateway Bagels on a near-daily basis. Supposedly to "pick up a few things," but really just to make sure Jonny was showing up for work (so far, so good). The end result was the house was fully stocked with bagels and four different flavors of cream cheese (jalapeño was most popular by a landslide, though Ernesto also had a soft spot for maple raisin walnut). Mary wasn't complaining.

Oh, and Griffin Connelly was dead to her. *I'll never again be friends with him*, she silently vowed.

Chantel had texted again, eager to get together. And even though Mary wasn't supposed to like Chantel, she couldn't deny the fact that, well, she did. Chantel was nice and maybe a little perfect, but she was perfect in a nice way. With Griff out of the picture, and Alexis and Chrissie away, Mary's social life wasn't bursting with excitement. She decided to meet up with Chantel, but making sure it was at a remote location. The fewer witnesses, the better. It wouldn't be good if word got out.

"Do you play tennis?" Chantel asked.

"I suck, but sure—just don't slaughter me," Mary said.

They met at the high school courts, which were usually empty in late August. Mary actually enjoyed playing. She represented decently enough and was quick to the ball, whereas Chantel tended to stay at the baseline and power away with a heavy forehand. They didn't keep score. After an hour, they'd worked up a sweat and sat on the bench under the shade, swigging from water bottles.

"Whoa," Mary gasped, shaking her head. "I need to do that more often. I'm out of shape."

"You're good for someone who never plays," Chantel said.

"Too many marshmallows," Mary quipped. "I should probably start eating kale instead, then I'd kill you."

"Yeah, right," Chantel joked.

"How was the no-phones thing at camp?" Mary asked. "Was it hard?"

Chantel leaned back. "No, not really. The first couple of days, you reach for it out of habit, but after a while you get used to it. Honestly, I liked it. You know what? I even wrote letters."

"Letters!" Mary joked. "What are those?"

"It's like email with paper, strange, I know," Chantel quipped. "I enjoyed reading them. Getting mail was special. Hakeem wrote to me—twice."

"You guys are still—"

Chantel threw up her hands, beaming. "I don't know what we are!"

"But you're like . . . progressing?"

"Progressing," Chantel laughed. "That sounds awful. Like a report card! No, we're just getting to know each other. Slowly. There's no hurry."

"So no pics," Mary said.

Chantel blushed. "Some, a little, but nothing, you know, exposed."

"Good," Mary said. "This is good."

"But I have to tell you something," Chantel said, leaning closer. "Promise you won't tell."

Mary nodded.

"I mean it," Chantel said. "Seriously."

"Okay, okay," Mary said, eager to hear what might come next.

"Hakeem told me he did get a picture—from Alexis."

"What?!"

"Yeah," Chantel said, mouth open, eyes twinkling.

"He told you that?"

"Last night," Chantel said.

"You got together last night?" Mary was working hard to keep up.

"We went climbing at the indoor rock gym, so much fun," Chantel said. "Anyway, I think he was shocked. We were together, his phone dinged, and there she was—topless!"

"Get out!"

"Well, she had her arms, you know, like this"—Chantel folded her arms in an X across her chest—"so nothing showed."

"What did Hakeem say?" Mary asked. "Were you mad?"

Chantel looked away, leaning her chin into her hand. "He says that he never asked, she just sent it out of nowhere. I told him to delete it."

"That's so wild," Mary said. Her mind reeled, thinking back to Alexis's announcement at the beach. She liked Hakeem. He was her next target. It must be true. "Are you sure you believe that Hakeem is innocent in all this? It sounds fishy."

Chantel began packing away the tennis balls, zipping the racket into the protective case. "I know how it sounds, but I do believe him," she said. "You had to be there, I guess. He was shocked. He didn't try to hide it from me."

"Are you going to say anything?" Mary asked.

Chantel laughed. "What am I going to say? Nice boobs?"

In that moment of sharing, Mary almost told Chantel to be careful. About how Chrissie and Alexis didn't plan on being her friends anymore. She thought about Griffin, and her brother Jonny. But for some reason, Mary didn't say a word. She kept those secrets to herself.

23
[floating]

IT WAS SUCH A CALMING SHADE OF BLUE-GREEN.
Soothing, peaceful. Mary drifted on an inflatable pool
mattress, her head hanging facedown in the water,
wearing goggles and a snorkel. She gazed deeply at
the bottom of Chrissie's pool and thought of all the
names she remembered from acrylic paint tubes and
other places: turquoise, olive, emerald, cadmium,
mint, lime, sea foam, lagoon, teal. She settled on
aquamarine, which was basically green with a bluish
tint. It was the color of the pool that she was absorbing into her bloodstream through her eyes. A serenity
seeping into her body. Mary had earrings that were

aquamarine gemstones, a color she avoided during the gray winter months. But for August afternoons in the blistering sun? Perfection.

Chrissie and Alexis were lounging side by side, content to find themselves returned home after thirteen epic days on the Jersey Shore. Upon seeing their friend Mary again, they squeezed her tight and said all the best, gushy things—but Mary sensed the connection between the two girls was stronger than ever. They were rock-solid besties, and nothing would come between that. Their bond felt like a wall through which Mary could never pass. To her surprise, it upset Mary to feel like an outcast. It wasn't logical, but a feeling was a feeling, not subject to notions of "right" or "wrong." Some unspoken part of her simply wanted to belong. She'd felt sad lately and wasn't sure why. Maybe it was just everything. So she floated on the water, letting her thoughts drift to that cruel idiot Griffin Connelly, and Chantel, and, always, Jonny.

Everyone said it was better that he was living on his own. Yet Mary's imagination kept her mind racing at night—a nervous, stressed feeling she couldn't push aside. She woke up in the morning and felt tired.

Everywhere she turned, Mary felt disconnected, as if she were fading into the background, as if she were absorbing the colors and designs of the carpets and wallpaper. Could she become a ghost, too? How come no one saw her, *really saw* her, anymore?

Mary felt increasingly invisible in her own home, a chameleon morphing into the background. There was a movie Ernesto had told her about, something about body snatchers, where pods grew in people's basements, garden sheds, attics. Eventually the pods slipped in and took the ordinary person's place. It's not like the pods killed the regular people—it was more of a transformation. The movie didn't make total sense, at least in Ernesto's retelling. You had to go with it, Mary guessed. A lot of movies were that way. Anyway, the pod change was a gradual unbe-coming, an unraveling of self, but mostly it was like death, because the original person—we'll call her Mary, for example—just slowly disappeared like a shadow drifting across a meadow into the dusky woods beyond. Mary longed for the start of school, the busyness of classes and crowded hallways, the sea of faces and the routine of nightly homework. A new beginning, a student's annual do-over. The summer was too long, too hard. She thought of the boy on the basketball court, his sleeveless shirt and thick eyebrows. That ball thumping on the asphalt like a heartbeat. Or did that rhythm come from within the cage of her own chest?

Water splashed on Mary's back. She lifted her head. It was Alexis, kneeling at the edge of the pool. She smiled, flashing a tidy row of white teeth. "Are you going to stay in there forever, Mary? Chrissie's mom brought out wraps for lunch. Come join us, sweetie. We have so much to talk about."

Chrissie laid out a colorful quilt, and the friends picnicked on the grass. Wraps and grapes and homemade brownies. A cold pitcher of sweetened iced tea to wash it all down. "You should have seen the house, Mary, it was sick!" Alexis gushed. "There were, like, I don't know how many rooms. Outdoor decks on three different levels. You should have come—it was huge."

Should have come? That was an annoying thing to say. Mary wasn't invited.

Alexis prattled on, talking about hipster-themed restaurants and hot tubs and swimming in the ocean at night. "It's so scary, the way the dark waves roll in, but I loved it so much. The stars twinkling in the night sky, so freaking gorgeous. Have you ever swum in the ocean at night?"

Mary had not.

"You should," Alexis said.

"Maybe someday," Mary replied. Her mood was flat. She wasn't being any fun. What was wrong with her?

"And what about you?" Chrissie asked.

"Kind of boring, quiet," Mary answered. "My brother moved out, which is good, I guess. Definitely less drama. And I made a couple of paintings that are pretty good."

"You're so talented," Alexis cooed.

Mary paused to look at her for a moment, wondering if there would be anything else. Like what the paintings were about or what they looked like. But nothing. Mary told them about hanging out with Griffin and his friends—and without going into details, how she definitely wasn't into him anymore.

Alexis squinched her nose in sympathy. "He doesn't seem like your type. What about Pat? He has potential."

Mary made a face, signaling she didn't have any interest in Pat or matchmaking in general. "How's Project Hakeem coming along?" she asked, shifting the conversation into new territory. "I suppose you couldn't make much progress while you were away."

Chrissie exchanged a look with Alexis. "I wouldn't say that."

"We've been communicating," Alexis admitted. "And, actually, there's a snag."

"With Chantel," Chrissie said.

"We have an idea," Alexis stated.

"But we need your help," Chrissie said.

Whoa. Now they were finishing each other's sentences like a pair of psychic twins. And if that wasn't weird enough, now they had concocted some kind of diabolical, mad-scientist plan. "Okay," Mary said. Not an okay that meant yes. It was more an okay that meant, *okay, I'm listening.*

Except Alexis and Chrissie didn't hear it that way. They heard agreement.

"Oh good!" Alexis said.

"We knew you'd save us!" Chrissie said, unexpectedly lurching forward to give a hug at the same time Mary was reaching for the grapes. They bumped heads. It kind of hurt, but Mary laughed to cover the pain.

Mary asked, "What's the problem with Chantel?"

"She's been flirting with Hakeem," Chrissie said. "Sending him pictures, the works. It's out of bounds."

Mary blinked, trying to take it in. "I'm surprised. Are you sure?"

"We know what we know," Chrissie said.

Alexis nodded. "We need to teach her a lesson."

"I don't—" Mary held up her hands. "Like how?"

"We were thinking. You know how she has that goldfish pond in her backyard?" Alexis said.

"Yeah, I think so," Mary said. "Orange carp."

"She loves those fish—it's so stupid," Chrissie said.

"What if we . . . did something to it?" Alexis wondered.

Mary sat in silence, deciding if they were serious. Did something? Chrissie looked at Mary, waiting.

"Wait, you want to kill some fish?" Mary asked.

Maybe it was the incredulous look on Mary's face. Or the shock of hearing those words out loud, spoken in that tone, bouncing back at them. It sounded awful, unthinkable—despite the fact that, obviously, they had already thought about it. Alexis pulled both hands through her hair, "No, no! That's a terrible idea. We're totally not killing fish!"

Chrissie snorted, "Of course not, ha, ha!"

"Because that would be, like, serial killer–type behavior," Mary said. "Jeffrey Dahmer stuff."

"Who's that?" Chrissie asked. "Is he in our grade?"

"Some guy who killed people and ate them," Mary said. "He had issues. There's a graphic novel and a movie."

"Cool," Chrissie said.

Mary blinked at that response. A slow blink, like one of those old dolls that clicked when you shut the eyes. Eyes open, shut, pause, open again. Performed with the dim hope that the world would be different when she opened her eyes.

"Oh yeah, we'd never," Alexis said.

"But still," Chrissie pointed out. "We've got to send a message. Because Chantel's out of control. I mean, it's just wrong. Alexis likes Hakeem. You don't do that to a friend."

Mary looked away, leaned away, wished she was far away. The girls may have sensed her doubt.

"Wait, are you on her side?" Chrissie asked.

"No, I mean, I love you guys," Mary said. "I'm

not as experienced with boy stuff as you. It's confusing, I guess."

"Not to me," Alexis said.

"We could ask Griffin to help us?" Chrissie suggested, turning to Alexis.

"What?" Mary said, alarmed. "Forget it, he'd make everything so much worse."

"Good," Alexis said. "We know you'll help us think of something, Mary. You're so smart."

"She's obsessed with pigs," Chrissie offered.

And that part, at least, was true. Mary wasn't so sure about the rest. Chantel did have a thing for pigs. A montage of pig images—photos of pigs on farms, in addition to cartoon character pigs such as Porky, Miss Piggy, Peppa, Hamm, and Sir Oinks-A-Lot—covered one wall of Chantel's bedroom. She had a huge, pink pig pillow complete with a curly tail. Chantel had pig plush toys, too. And, come to think of it, her all-time favorite book was *Charlotte's Web*, featuring the greatest pig of all, Wilbur.

"She's a pig!" Alexis said harshly.

"I think she thinks they're cute," Mary offered defensively.

"Well, if she's going to send pictures to Hakeem,

maybe we should send pictures of our own," Chrissie said. "You are good at Photoshop, aren't you, Mary?"

Mary couldn't think of an answer.

Chrissie looked at Alexis, who said, "That's okay. Never mind. We'll handle it."

24

[crystals]

MARY WAS HAPPY WHEN HER MOTHER KNOCKED ON her door with the offer to make blueberry pancakes.

"Do we have chocolate chips?" Mary asked, instantly perking up.

Ernesto wasn't around that morning. A friend's tree had fallen, knocking down a fence, and he went over first thing with his tools and pickup truck. "He loves that chainsaw more than me," Mary's mother said, still wrapped in a scarlet bathrobe, flipping pancakes while bacon sizzled in the iron griddle. Mary gulped down a glass of orange juice, slowly waking to the smells of Saturday morning.

"I was wondering if you'd like to go shopping today? Do you have free time?" Mrs. O'Malley asked. "I saw they came out with the back-to-school lists. Lord knows I've already purchased enough folders to last a lifetime. And you do need some new clothes. Growing too fast."

Free time was something that Mary had in excess these days. Alexis and Chrissie were both trying out for cheerleading—they'd make it, easy—and, besides, Mary still wasn't completely over the icky feeling she got the last time they were together. She'd seen photos on Instagram last night of a six-girl sleepover–slash–birthday party at Tamara Agee's. It didn't make Mary jealous—honestly, the party didn't look like all that much fun, except for the cupcakes, and she wasn't that tight with Tamara, so it was all understandable—but it still left Mary feeling detached.

A floating-alone-in-the-clouds feeling.

The chocolate chip pancakes with warm maple syrup helped.

As far as the plot against Chantel, Mary decided to do nothing. She wouldn't participate. She'd stand by and let whatever happened, happen. Which was probably nothing, she told herself. Chantel would be fine. It was nice to think so.

Mary's mom had this habit that when she drove, she put on a big show about putting away her phone. You know, modeling positive behaviors! But if it dinged, she always reached for it. "I'm just glancing," she'd say, aware of Mary's disapproval. "I'd never send a text."

"I've seen you do it," Mary said.

"At red lights, stop signs, maybe," her mother said.

It dinged and Mary said, "Want me to read it?"

"No, no, that's fine," Mrs. O'Malley insisted. She grabbed the phone and held it in her right hand for the rest of the trip, as if she were protecting it from desperadoes.

Mary found the mall a humorous place. She liked eating in the food court (an unexplainable weakness for Arby's) and watching the people. She still remembered watching an entire family—mother, father, and three children—all in matching L.L.Bean jackets. The bubbly kind. Same color, same everything. Even better, they were each eating Auntie Anne's pretzels. People were weird, and there was nothing like the mall to drive that message home.

"Hold on, I have to take this," Mrs. O'Malley said, indicating the phone. She walked to a less trafficked area and leaned against the wall, her back to Mary. Ten minutes later, she was back—and Mary was annoyed.

"I thought you wanted to do this," Mary said. "It was your plan."

"I know, but—Mary, you have no idea."

"It's Jonny, right?"

Mrs. O'Malley's lips tightened. She studied the ceiling lights and nodded. "There's a problem with the deposit check, among other things. It's not your concern. Come on. Show me those boots you've been talking about."

"Is he going to be okay?" Mary asked.

An anguished look crossed her mother's face—it happened fast, then it was over, and she was back to normal again—but Mary knew what she had seen. The worry and strain. The inability to give a good answer.

So they sat there at the mall and talked about it as people came and went, carrying shopping bags and guzzling gigantic neon smoothies. "I don't know if he's going to be okay," Mary's mother admitted. "We're doing everything we can to help him."

Mary locked eyes with her mother. "Like kicking him out of the house?"

"Oh, Mary," Mrs. O'Malley said, placing a hand on her daughter's back. "I wish I had all the answers. It's been so hard for everyone, including your brother. You get mad at me for staring at the phone. And you're right. I'm trying—I am trying, Mary—to be better. But every time it vibrates, my heart stops. I think it's going to be bad news, terrible news." She looked down at her lap, her chest heaving.

"Should he go somewhere?" Mary said. "One of those rehab places?"

"He has to want to," her mother said. "Really want to. I believe that it can't be forced on him. Jonny has to have a voice in these big decisions, or else it won't work. And right now, as crazy as this sounds, he thinks he's doing okay."

"He's not," Mary said.

"He thinks he can manage it. He says he wants to quit on his own, maybe later. Those for-profit rehab facilities"—she shook her head—"I don't know. They aren't for everyone. I've set him up with a therapist. But now he's got to go and put in the effort. That's an important step. He's agreed to consider taking medication that will help him feel better, avoid what he calls the Black Fog, maybe not have the same strong urges."

"What kind of medicine?" Mary asked.

"Mary, listen to me," Mrs. O'Malley said. "Your brother has a substance use problem. Those drugs he's been taking rewire the brain. He's been using all kinds of things—alcohol, pills, cocaine, I'm not sure what else—for a few years now. He was doing it in our home, down the hall from your bedroom. I can't have that. I can't."

"But what about him?" Mary asked. She felt upset. Mary looked away, blinked, determined not to shed tears.

Her mother touched Mary's bare leg. Her hand felt as light and welcome as a ladybug. "I've been reading. Talking to friends, experts. I'm trying to take better care of myself so I can take better care of the people I love."

Mary nodded, wiped her face.

"I tell Jonny that he's throwing his life away," she said, "but these past years, I've been doing the exact same thing. I've been worried sick every day, not paying enough attention to you. And I've learned that I can't control if drugs are going to destroy his life. But I promise you, Mary, they will not destroy ours."

They sat on that bench as if they were alone on a mountaintop. Just the two of them, locked in a long embrace. Mrs. O'Malley got up, walked away, returned with a big box of malted milk balls. And when they felt better, they shopped. "Retail therapy," Mary's mother called it. Mary did pretty well: two skirts, some tops, and the coolest boots in town. Not cheap, either.

Mrs. O'Malley paused before a crystal store, staring at the display window. The store was filled with healing stones and crystals, incense and essential oils, little Buddha figurines and spiritual books—it was that kind of place. A recording of songbirds played on the store speaker system. Mrs. O'Malley browsed inside for a while, and Mary didn't even complain about the musty incense smell that lingered in the air and probably stunk up her clothes. But on the way out, Mary said, "Mom, I think it's great if that stuff helps you. I won't judge. Just one thing. Please don't become one of those people who buys rocks at the mall for twenty-five dollars, okay?"

Mrs. O'Malley stopped in her tracks and laughed out loud. "I'm sorry, Mary, but no promises!"

"Some of the crystals are kind of pretty," Mary admitted.

Together they walked hand in hand toward whatever came next.

25
[school]

MARY NOTICED THE NEW BOY, ERIC, IN HOME BASE ON the first day of school. This was a positive development. Home base was a free period, monitored by reasonably cool, bald-shaven Mr. Scofield, who pretty much let everybody do what they wanted so long as they weren't disruptive. Once the school year kicked into gear, most kids used home base to catch up on sleep or homework or phone time. But on the first day of school, it was mostly lively chatter and lots of hugs. That was a thing that drove Mary a little nuts: all the hugging. It felt false, an empty show without substance.

Mary was chatting with the girls in the back,

swapping schedules and stories about their summers, when she looked over and there he was. Eric sat by himself, head down, pretending to be absorbed in a paperback. Mary could see that his eyes roved around, slyly checking out the new faces. She couldn't blame him. It had to be hard to be the new kid in a big, loud school like BCMS.

Behind him and two rows over, she caught sight of David Hallenback. She couldn't help but wonder if he was ever able to run a full mile. Kind of doubted it. Oh well. Not every thought that pops into your head is the kindest. You have to sort through them, discard the worst, Mary figured. Hallenback was a loner, unpopular and still basically a little boy. Seventh grade was curious that way. A mish-mash between elementary and high school. Some kids rocketed past puberty—became boys with muscles and girls with curves—while many others hadn't made the leap yet. David was still one of them.

Mary saw that Hallenback was staring with an intense expression of contempt. Eyes blazing, brow furrowed. She followed his gaze and recognized the target of his anger: it was Eric, the new boy.

But why?

Hallenback's hostility gave Mary a brief, uneasy feeling. The moment passed, Mary glanced away, and he was again just another curly-haired kid without a clue. Even so, Mary felt a chill, convinced she had glimpsed something awful and damaged beneath the surface. His gentle public mask had fallen away. There was anger beneath it all.

After attendance, Mary boldly slid into an empty seat beside Eric. With a tilt of her head, Mary indicated Hallenback and confided, "I wouldn't talk to that kid if I was you."

Eric looked at her—wearing jeans and a light-colored shirt that showed off her tan—and his eyes widened in recognition. "You were with those guys that day." He glanced back at Hallenback. "And that's the kid you were following, right?"

Mary stretched, raising her arms to the ceiling. On the court, Eric had told Griff that he didn't see anyone. Now he just confirmed that it wasn't true. He'd seen Hallenback after all. Eric wasn't a practiced liar. A good quality, she decided.

"So you lied, huh? I knew it."

"I didn't want any drama," Eric replied.

Mary studied him closely. Eric was soft-spoken,

almost shy. Maybe it was left over from the awkwardness of their initial meeting out on the court. Or just first-day jitters. He seemed nice, though, with bright blue eyes, and confident in a quiet way.

Eric asked, "Did he do something wrong?"

Mary leaned closer and advised, "Just steer clear."

Eric cast another furtive glance at Hallenback. "Considering the way he looks at me, that's not going to be a problem. I don't think he likes me."

No, Mary thought, *he definitely doesn't.* And it puzzled her. Why would Hallenback have an issue with the new kid? Eric didn't do anything to him. Except, maybe . . . he was a witness to Hallenback's humiliation. Covered in ketchup. Maybe seeing Eric brought back all that embarrassment.

Mary, too, felt a similar regret surrounding that day. Eric associated her with that afternoon on the basketball court. Mary and Griff's crew. She wasn't proud of that connection. They talked a little more. Eric told her he didn't own a cell phone, which was different. That's not how things normally worked in this town. Maybe he was one of those kids from a "progressive" home, where there's no TV, everyone's a vegan, and the father wears a beard like a wizard.

"I'll see you around," Mary said, not wanting to linger any longer. Already eyes from the back of the room were upon them. But before stepping away she felt compelled to say, "Just so you know, I wasn't part of it that day on the basketball court."

Eric raised his eyebrows. "Seemed like you were."

"I don't hang out with them anymore," Mary said. It was important that he knew that. "I'm not like that."

Eric nodded, not meeting her eyes. If he believed her, Mary couldn't tell.

Lunch was the next hurdle of the day, marking a clear hierarchy of the social order. Everyone staking out groups and tables, people and places. Mary had successfully avoided Chantel for the remainder of the summer. They texted a bit, in short bursts, but Mary made excuses whenever getting together came up. Chantel had soccer and AAU basketball and strict parents, so the cooling of their friendship wasn't that dramatic. At least, Mary didn't think so, until they almost literally bumped into each other in the cafeteria. Mary turned and Chantel stopped short, almost spilling a lunch tray on Mary's shirt. "Oh, hey!" Mary said in surprise.

"Hi," Chantel answered. There was no warmth in her insincere smile.

They looked at each other awkwardly, close enough to touch and yet a million miles away. Chantel saw something over Mary's shoulder, lifted her chin in greeting. "Save me a seat," she called out.

Mary looked back and saw a few sporty girls gathering at a long table. Everyone busy staking a claim to their place in the pecking order. "Here we are, seventh grade," Mary said. "We made it."

"Um-hmmm," Chantel replied. "I'm gonna—"

"Sure, sure," Mary said, stepping aside to let Chantel pass.

And that was it. No one had to say a word of explanation. It was all understood. Mary hadn't done anything wrong. Not a single thing. She wasn't obligated to be friends with Chantel. People changed friend groups all the time. Why did it feel so uncomfortable? Mary took a seat next to Alexis, across from Tamara and Chrissie. Everyone was full of hugs and compliments. Mary's boots were a huge hit, even though it was technically too soon in the season to wear them. Tamara made a little joke about it.

"Did I see you talking with her?" Chrissie wanted to know.

"With who?"

"You know," Chrissie said. "Your friend."

Mary looked back over her shoulder. Chantel was looking the other way, telling a story with expressive hand gestures. "She's not," Mary answered flatly, wondering if it might actually be true.

Off by himself, Eric sat with the soggy company of a meatball sub and a bag of chips. Rookie mistake. Never, ever order the meatball sub. Griff walked over, standing by Eric's elbow like a shadow. They talked briefly. Griffin smiled, titled his head, turned to walk away. Eric stood and followed. He took a place at Griff's table, along with Cody, Droopy, Hakeem, Marshall, Sinjay, Will, and Pat. Mary's heart went cold. There was always someone willing to follow Griffin Connelly. Too bad Eric was one of those guys.

Mary was glad when the day ended and the final bell clanged, and she pedaled home by herself on the bicycle that Griffin had given her.

Only 179 more school days to go.

It would be a five marshmallow afternoon.

26

[wolves]

SATURDAY NIGHT AND AN EMPTY HOUSE. MARY WAS alone and loving the freedom and solitude. She could do anything she wanted—there was no one looking over her shoulder—and it was laughable to see what kind of everyday, normal, boring activities she chose. Mary made a big bowl of popcorn in the microwave. Read for a while. She thought about lounging on the couch and watching a scary movie, but it was already dark outside and she wasn't absolutely 100 percent sure she could handle the fear factor.

There were times when Mary wished she had a dog. Those times were morning, noon, and night, every single day of her life. But now, alone in her groaning, buzzing, creaking home—the house was never this loud when people were around—Mary strongly felt that lifetime desire. Dog as companion and protector. So she got a little spooked when at nine thirty there were voices at the front door, and sharp knocking.

"Little May, Little May, let us in!" Jonny roared. "Or with a huff . . . and a puff . . ." She heard laughter, giggling. He wasn't alone. She peeked out the window and saw a thin girl in a black skirt with stringy auburn hair and another boy she'd didn't recognize. He wore a big, loose afro and dark shades, which was ridiculous because, yeah, it was dark out. He puffed on a vape; Mary saw its glow intensify, then fade to black.

Mary stood by the closed door, watching the doorknob jiggle.

Jonny rapped against the door more forcefully. "Oh, May? Oh, my darling sister?"

"Mom's not home," Mary said through the door.

"May, I don't have a key," Jonny said. "Are you going to let us in or what?"

She heard voices and laughter. The other boy said

something about checking around the back. *Was the glass door locked?* Yes, Mary remembered. She'd locked every door and window. "Mom said not to let you inside," she said through the closed door. "I'm sorry."

"Mary, Jesus," Jonny snapped. "Just open the door."

Mary turned the lock, *click*, and stepped back.

The door swung open and Jonny tumbled inside, waving in his two companions. Mary backed up another step. A ripple of apprehension floated down her spine. "I'm alone," she repeated. "Are you here to pay back the money you owe me?"

"May-May, my sweet May!" Jonny said, opening his arms in greeting. "Vivvy, Dez, this is my little sister, May-May. Any food in the kitchen? Mom's always got good snacks. Ernesto loves those pretzel nuggets! We're starved, May, famished!"

Mary crossed her arms. Dez had a shabby, scarecrow-left-in-the-rain appearance, faded jeans and a rumpled shirt. Vivvy, who was surely Vivian Connelly, Griff's sister, had all the features of faded beauty: long, straight hair, narrow hips, slender shoulders—but with orange-blue discolorations on one arm, like she'd bumped into a brick wall. Mary decided by the looks of things that her brother was very much with the wrong crowd, and he fit in perfectly.

Vivvy and Dez glanced around, as if casing a bank for security cameras. They nodded in Mary's direction without ever looking her in the eyes. "There's some frozen pizza, I think," Mary offered.

"Where's the booze at?" Dez asked. He giggled softly. A joke that wasn't a joke. Vivian, who had Griff's same complexion and hair color, smacked Dez playfully and shushed him.

"Whoa, popcorn!" Jonny lurched at the bowl on the dining room table. He shoved a fistful into his mouth, dropping kernels to the floor. Mary's art supplies were spread out on the table.

"Jonny? Jonny!" Mary repeated, trying to get his attention. He seemed high on something, unfocused, giddy. "What's going on?"

He turned and, with some effort, focused on his sister. A crooked smile reached his lips. "May Queen! We decided to bring the party here."

"I don't think that's a good idea," Mary said.

Dez and Vivvy tottered toward the kitchen. Dez

paused at a photo on the wall, snickered as if it said something funny. A private joke. "That you, man?" he called to Jonny.

"What? Yeah, that's us, Cape Cod," Jonny replied, walking over to the framed photograph. "Long time ago, right, May? You must have just turned three. Our last vacation together with Mom and Dad." He scratched uncomfortably at the inside of his elbow. "Anyway, help yourself to whatever's in the kitchen, guys! I'll be in inna minute. Just need to"—he waggled a hand in the direction of the stairs—"get a few things."

He stomped up the stairs while the others walked loose-limbed into the kitchen, flicking on the lights and noisily opening cupboards and drawers. Mary stood as if under siege, not sure where to turn. Her phone was charging on the table. She unplugged it and slipped it into her back pocket. What should she do?

"How do you work this oven?" Vivian called. Mary hurried into the kitchen. Vivian Connelly had already placed a box of frozen pizza onto a baking rack, and was vacantly hovering a finger over the oven controls.

"Um, you were going to take it out of the box, right?" Mary said, as if talking to a child. She stepped in, gently brushed Viv aside, removed the pizza from the box, removed the plastic wrapper, and set the controls. "It should be ready in fifteen minutes," she told them, setting the timer.

Dez pulled out a box of cereal and had plunged his arm into it up to the elbow.

"We have bowls, spoons," Mary offered, voice dripping with snark. She made a silent note to discard the box after they left.

Dez kept chewing. He probably didn't realize she was talking. He seemed pretty absorbed in chewing, as if it required all his concentration.

Jonny thumped down the stairs.

He was carrying a Tiffany lamp and a shoebox.

"What are you doing?" Mary asked.

"I need this for my apartment," Jonny said.

"That was in Mom's room," Mary said. "I think it's expensive."

Jonny sniffed, rubbed his nose with the sleeve of his upper arm. "I hope so. Anyway, I need light. I can't sit in the dark, May. You guys have all this fancy stuff while I'm in a dingy hovel. Is that fair?"

"What's in there?" Mary asked, gesturing to the box.

"Baseball cards. I'm going to sell 'em," he said, sniffingly.

"Those were Dad's," Mary said. "You can't—"

"Calm down, May, it's not his ashes, it's just cardboard. I can get good money for these."

"His ashes," Mary repeated in disbelief. It felt like a punch to the gut.

Jonny stood, slightly wavering.

"You're gross. I hate you," Mary said. "Get out. Mom will be back any minute. You don't want to be here when—"

"She's in the city, seeing a play," Jonny said. "Mom won't be back for hours. How do you think I knew to come over here?"

"You're such a jerk," Mary said.

Jonny nodded, as if in agreement. He even smiled wanly, looking sad and stricken. Maybe somewhere deep down she had wounded him.

"Yo, look what I found," Dez cried, entering the room. He held up a quart-size bottle of liquor. "Rum from Jamaica, mon!"

"That's not yours," Mary protested.

"Your mom won't miss it," Dez told Jonny, ignoring Mary completely. "It was way, way in the back."

"Get out," Mary ordered.

Dez looked from Mary to Jonny. "What's up with this? You said she was cool."

"She is," Jonny murmured. He lowered his head, then perked up again, raising the lamp in triumph. "Let's go. I got what we needed."

"Score!" Vivvy celebrated, twirling car keys on her index finger. "Bye, bye, little sister. It's been real."

"You're driving?" Mary said in shock.

"No, we're going to walk five miles," Jonny said.

"Jog, maybe," Dez quipped, snickering again. It's what he did, Mary surmised, made unfunny comments and giggled like he was the only one deep enough to get the joke. Truly annoying. They tumbled out the door like leaves blown by some invisible wind. Mary turned the lock and leaned her back against the wall, breathing heavily, relieved they were gone. After a few minutes, the oven dinged.

Pizza was ready.

And there on the side table, Mary saw the shoe-box of baseball cards. Jonny had left them behind. Maybe he wasn't ready to sell those memories after all.

27

[junkie]

MARY HADN'T SAID MORE THAN TEN WORDS TO Griffin Connelly since the ketchup incident. They saw each other in the halls, locked eyes, but didn't speak or smile. No one in school would have detected any outward enmity—theirs was just your basic, standard freeze-out. It was just one more thing that added to the overall suckiness of seventh grade in September. Middle school blues: the trouble with Chantel, the weirdness within the shifting dynamics of her friend group, and bad vibes from the entire crew that hung around with Griff. It didn't leave a lot of options. No matter where Mary turned, nothing felt right.

She'd already bombed a science test and was lost in math—Ms. Parmeleit was the worst at explaining things, and she was an unbearable Yankees fan, constantly crowing about every last victory. Up to this year, Mary had aced her studies without effort. But things had changed.

Outside during recess, a loose gathering of students sat at the tables under the shade of a large, umbrella-shaped tree. Drew Peterson sauntered up to Mary's table with Will and Sinjay. "We ran into your brother last weekend."

Mary slowly turned her head in the direction of Droopy in a show of supreme indifference.

"It was messed up," the big, raw-boned boy continued. "Is your brother, like, homeless or something?" He had a sneering, mocking attitude in his delivery. "Jonny, right?"

Mary glanced at the others, assessing the mood. At least eight people had heard what he said. In middle school, that was as good as making announcements on the PA system. The whole world would know. Droopy had also gotten the attention of Alexis and Chrissie, who lived for this kind of playground gossip. "Don't you have somewhere to go?" Mary spat.

"It was scuzzy—he was with a couple of dirtbag friends. He asked if we knew you. What happened to him? They were smoking cigarettes and even tried to hit us up for money—I mean, we were all wondering, is your brother a junkie?"

"How do you even—" snapped Mary.

"Is that true, Mary?" Alexis asked.

"Oh, so true!" Droopy interjected, enjoying the spotlight. "Total human trash show. Cigarette butts, broken glass everywhere. We were, like, gone, you know, out of there. Bunch of dopeheads. I didn't want to be near that stuff. Griff told us they sniff heroin, maybe shoot it."

Griff told us, Mary noted. Was he the one pulling these strings? She felt the presence of eyes on her, waiting for a reaction. Mary shifted with embarrassment. A worm of shame crawled through her stomach. She found it hard to think. A dull roar, like the drone of a jet engine, filled her head.

Chrissie reached out, squeezed Mary's hand.

"That's enough, be gone," Alexis said, flicking a wrist at the boys.

"We want to be alone with our girl," Chrissie said.

Mary appreciated their support. They could be

really nice at times. A moment later, Mary got up to leave. "I've got to, um," she stammered. "The nurse's office."

"Are you okay?" Chrissie asked. "Do you want us to come with you?"

Mary didn't answer. She just blindly hurried away, bent slightly forward, holding her stomach. She muttered something about the nurse's office and barreled past Mrs. Rosen, the trim and tidy lunch aide, who wisely let Mary go. When kids held their stomachs and moaned about the nurse's office, Mrs. Rosen knew to get out of the way. It wasn't her first rodeo.

Claiming a killer migraine (which always worked) and a mother too busy with work at the bank to pick her up, Mary managed to spend the rest of the school day in the nurse's office. She lay on a cot in a darkened space, an aromatic towel draped across her forehead. She felt humiliated about Jonny, and at the same time she hated herself for letting it get to her. Why was she so afraid and embarrassed? As if what Drew Peterson thought meant anything to her. And yet, there it was: she couldn't even rise up in defense of her only brother. He had called Jonny "human trash" and a "junkie," and she just sat there in stunned silence and shame.

Mary's thoughts bounced around like bumper cars the rest of the day, so that when it was time to go, she felt foggy and uncertain. Not wanting to look at another face, Mary lingered until the buses left and most of the walkers departed. She distractedly fumbled with the lock at the bike racks when she heard a voice. "Everything okay?"

Mary turned and saw the school cop, Officer Goldsworthy, standing nearby. He often circulated outside at the end of the school day, saw the buses off, kept a low-key eye on the comings and goings. Mary realized she'd been crying, burbling like a baby while spinning the combination lock round in circles. No wonder he checked on her. In response, Mary wiped her eyes. "Fine, I'm good," she said, looking at her feet. "Really."

Technically the school's resource officer, Officer Goldsworthy was a cop who'd been assigned to the middle school. He was an intimidating presence, a large black man who always looked physically constrained in a suit and necktie, but Mary had never seen him do anything other than talk quietly to people. A lot of big guys were like that. They didn't have to "do" anything, because nobody dared test them.

There, Mary finally got the lock. She wrapped the chain loosely around the seat pole and rolled the bike out of the rack. He was still there, watching.

"That's a nice bicycle, Mary. Is it new?"

He knew her name. Okay, that was unexpected.

"I borrowed it from a friend," she answered.

Officer Goldsworthy nodded. "That's a nice friend."

A short laugh leaped from Mary's throat. "Not really."

He laughed, too, and asked, "How's your brother doing?"

Oh hell, not now. Mary wasn't up for this. She snapped on the strap of the bicycle helmet. "He's . . ."

And that's all her mouth could manage. Her vocal cords glitched. The words wouldn't come.

"I'm sorry," the officer said. "I'll leave you alone. Maybe we'll talk another time." He turned to step away and stopped himself. He loitered for a few seconds, nodding, looking off at the clouds. "I'm rooting for him. You tell Jonny that for me. I'm rooting for all of you."

"You know him?"

"I do," Officer Goldsworthy said, stepping closer. "I remember Jonny when he went here. We talked sometimes. I played football for Clemson, back when I had two good knees. Jonny liked asking me about that. And I've seen him since."

Mary looked at the man. Without thinking, she blurted, "Some jerk called him a junkie today. That's why I was crying."

The man took that in, gave it some thought.

"Is that what you call him?" he asked.

Mary shook her head. "He's my brother."

Officer Goldsworthy scratched the side of his face. He wore a big, gold ring. "At the force, we're trying to get away from that kind of language. It's degrading and demeaning. Junkie. Druggie. Crackhead. Addict. It dehumanizes the victims of this disease."

Mary listened, swallowed. Her throat felt dry.

"There's too much blame and not enough compassion," the man said. "I don't think calling people names helps us face the problem, do you?"

Mary's eyes supplied him with her answer.

"I'm sorry, I don't mean to preach," he said. "That's something I got from my father, the good

Reverend Goldsworthy. But this is an issue I care about a great deal. We see a lot of it around here, more than you'd expect. The EMTs, you don't want to hear their stories. It's the hidden disease. People don't like to talk about it. The shame and the suffering. We've lost too many lives already."

Mary didn't speak. There wasn't anything to say.

And then, in parting, the man offered up five simple words, like a priest at the altar in a high-ceilinged church: "Your brother's a good kid."

Mary watched him walk toward the front doors, feeling the echo of his words reverberate in her chest. *He was*, she thought. Maybe he always will be. Mary pushed the bike back into the rack, left it unlocked, dumped the helmet on the ground, and walked home. She'd never ride that bike again. Three days later, it was gone.

28
[paella]

ERNESTO HAD BEEN SPENDING MORE TIME AT THE house, which didn't bother Mary. He did something subtle that Mary observed but couldn't quite figure out. Her mom was happier, lighter, but that wasn't it. Everything just went smoother, like in science when she experimented with friction and gravity. Mary recalled sliding blocks of wood down a ramp. Each identical block was covered with different surfaces: aluminum foil, ordinary wood, and sandpaper. The aluminum foil slid down easily, the regular block came next, while the sandpaper required a lot more gravity.

Ernesto, she realized, was aluminum foil.

Less friction.

He cooked that night for the first time in their house, and Mary helped. It was fun. They made a traditional paella dish that Ernesto said he learned from his grandmother, who immigrated from Spain long ago.

"First a sprinkle of salt into the pan, then the olive oil," Ernesto instructed. He prepared the chicken—which was gross, not Mary's thing—and had Mary fry it in the pan. When the chicken was almost ready, he asked her to open space in the middle of the pan for the vegetables, lima beans, and other greens. With flair, Ernesto added the seasonings. "I never measure," he said, scoffing at the thought. "A good cook does it by taste." He threw in sweet paprika and grated tomato and garlic. Mary stirred it all together, breathing in the rich aroma. Ernesto poured in chicken stock and two pinches of saffron, bringing it all to a boil.

"I didn't know you knew how to cook," Mary said.

"Ah, this is simple. I've lived alone many years. Look at my belly—I do okay, no? But today I miss my pots and pans. A good cook wants an iron skillet,

Mary, not this fake Teflon stuff. It flakes off, you die, cancer, boom. What good is that? And these flimsy knives," he said, making a face, "very sad."

Mary's mother, laughing from a seat at the table, said, "You should bring your knives here, if mine make you want to cry."

Ernesto turned to her, "If you'd like."

It felt to Mary like she was witnessing a moment. They were talking about knives, but it was bigger than that. A merging of cutlery, of lives. "What now?" she asked.

"The rice!" Ernesto exclaimed. He poured it into the pan. "No more stirring, Mary. Give your arm a rest. Now we let it cook. You can set the table, if you don't mind. And pour your splendid mother more wine." Ernesto adjusted the flame to a simmer with painstaking precision.

"Pay attention, Mary. I like the rice to be a little burnt, sticking to the bottom of the pan," he said, a trick his grandmother had taught him. "Some lemon and—perfection!"

The meal was a happy one, and delicious. They didn't talk about Jonny. And Mary noticed that her mother never once checked her phone.

"But what a mess you've made of my kitchen!" Mary's mother teased.

"No, no, you sit," Ernesto said when the meal was finished. "I actually like to clean."

Mrs. O'Malley looked at Mary, raising her eyebrows and flashing a discreet thumbs-up. Mary grinned. "Mom, maybe you should show Ernesto where we keep the vacuum."

Later, snuggling together on the living room couch, Mary told her mother about what happened at school and her conversation with Officer Goldsworthy. Mrs. O'Malley rubbed Mary's back while she listened.

"We have so much to learn." Mary's mother got up and returned with a few pamphlets. "Here's some information I got from the therapist. I should have involved you sooner. Maybe we can go together one day. All of us. A family session. I think it will help."

She continued, "Your brother has a damaged brain. Think of it as a broken leg. It's not that he's 'bad' or 'weak' or 'selfish.' Yes, he's made mistakes—it's true. Haven't we all? But now the drugs have impaired the way his brain processes information. It's like his wiring is all screwed up. The signals and messages aren't right. Even if Jonny sincerely wants to get on the road to recovery, it's likely not going to be a smooth, straight line—there may be relapses, bad scenes."

"Like the other night," Mary said.

"I'm very sorry you had to go through that," she answered. "I've tried to protect you from it. Maybe that was another of my mistakes. I do that a lot. But this is our life now. We don't get to pick our stories. And I think for you—and for me—we're going to have to learn how to carry this weight." She reached out with two fingers and lifted Mary's chin. "Head high, chin up."

Mary felt a small change happening within her. As if a chrysalis had formed deep in her belly. Some new miracle would emerge. Not only a new way of thinking about her brother, but a new way of feeling about everything, and everyone. She silently promised herself that no matter what, she would never again feel ashamed of Jonny. Pissed off, maybe. Angry, hurt, disappointed, sure. But not ashamed.

"Did he ever find his phone?" Mary asked.

"The one he supposedly lost?"

Mary allowed a new thought to enter her mind. Maybe Jonny didn't lose it. Maybe he sold it. She had to remember not to believe him. To love, but not to trust. It was confusing.

Mrs. O'Malley took a long, slow breath. "I bought him a cheap phone. Just so he can receive calls, text. That's something I insisted on. We have to have a way to stay in contact. Especially if he needs us, ever, for any reason."

"That's smart," Mary said. "Same number?"

"Yes, same number," Mary's mother answered.

Mary fell asleep early that night before ten o'clock. It had been a day, and her stomach was full. But a voice awakened her in the middle of the night. "Jonny?" she said, sitting up, expecting to see him by the side of the bed. But no one was there, just the lingering sound of his voice in her ears. Must have been dreaming. She picked up the phone to check the time. It was 3:37.

He was in trouble somewhere.

Mary punched in a message, writing to him by his old nickname: *Jonny Bear.*

He answered, amazingly, thirty seconds later. *May Queen.*

And that was enough. He was alive, somewhere

in the night, and they were connected by a gossamer thread.

What are you doing up? he wrote.

Mary yawned, typed, *Going back to bed now.*

I'm sorry, he wrote. *My little May.*

Shhh, she answered.

I'm so sorry, he wrote again, five minutes later. *You deserve better than me.*

But she had already fallen back to sleep.

29
[empathy]

MARY SAW ERIC IN SCHOOL DURING HOME BASE, lunch, and last period—English. They managed to talk a little, exchange a few words, every day. She noticed that he kept an eye on her, and she was pleased by the attention. They sometimes traveled the same pathways from class to class, silently in close proximity. Mary began to treasure these little moments of nearness. Nothing earth-shattering, just a growing ease in each other's presence.

"Still no phone," Mary teased, leaning on his desk in home base.

"Nope, but I do own a guitar," Eric said, looking up at her, his blue eyes shining.

"Okay, maybe that beats a phone," Mary said. "Are you any good?"

"No, I suck," he said, laughing. "Every time I pick it up, it's a knife fight—and the guitar kicks my butt every single time."

Mary suspected it wasn't true. He wasn't the kind of kid who'd brag. If he was good, Eric wouldn't say so. They talked about what kind of music they liked. Mary didn't know many of the groups he mentioned, but she nodded at the familiar names. "I guess I'm more into radio stuff." She named a popular hit song. "Do you like it?" A straight-up question.

"It's okay, I guess," Eric replied with hesitation.

Mary smiled, leaned closer. "I think it's insanely bad. Makes my ears bleed."

"Whew, I didn't want to say," Eric admitted.

"In case I liked it?"

"In case you loved it," he answered. "It would have cast doubt on the future of our, you know, friendship."

Mary heard it, the slight catch in his voice. By the

look on his face, she guessed he didn't intend to say it. Not the words so much, but the tentative, vulnerable way the words fell from his lips. She answered, "I'm glad to hear I passed the test."

So, yeah, she was putting that out there.

"I wouldn't go that far—it was just a quiz," Eric joked.

"Talking about music makes me think of my brother," Mary said.

Eric looked baffled. "Because . . . why?"

"He always used to have a passionate opinion about everything—and he was always right. I mean, sometimes I would like a song, but I wouldn't know why. I'm not super sophisticated about music. I like what I like, and that's as far as it goes. But Jonny—that's my brother, but you guessed that—he would lay it all out in excruciating detail, and explain exactly why some song I liked was the worst song ever in the history of western civilization. In the most hysterical and cruel way!" Mary laughed, remembering how smart and caustically funny he could be. "A cheesy song filled with clichés would make him so angry. He'd snap pencils in half, throw things. But mostly, my brother would make me come into his room and tell me what I had to listen to—like, right that second, he'd cue up a song, wrap the headphones around my head. I was this little girl, third grade maybe, and he'd be, like, 'You must listen to this tune by the Ramones!'"

"Sounds like you love him," Eric observed.

"Does it?" Mary asked, as surprised as if a wombat had suddenly waddled into the classroom. She hadn't expected to be talking about her brother, recalling good times. Mary thought it over. "Yeah, I pretty much used to flat-out worship him."

"Used to."

"What?"

"Past tense," Eric said.

"Things changed," Mary admitted, glancing at the wall clock. Some shift in the room alerted her that time was almost up. People packing up, tucking papers in folders. Fourth period next. "He's just . . . different now. My brother loves only one thing."

Eric grinned. "Yeah? Like what? Bavarian polka music?"

"Getting wasted," Mary replied.

"Oh."

That lowered the temperature fast.

"He has a problem with addiction," Mary said, immediately regretting the language. "I guess I should say, he has a substance use disorder. It's like he has a broken leg in his brain. He gets mixed-up signals. Something about dopamine, chemicals in the brain, frontal lobes—I don't understand it completely." It was the first time she'd confessed those things to anyone other than her mother. Something about Eric made it feel safe, that she could trust this blond-haired boy with her secrets. She could be her true self.

Eric looked pensive. It was one of his endearing features, the way he'd ruminate deeply before speaking, arranging his thoughts in perfect order, like the Thanksgiving dinner table before company arrived. Napkins, plates, candles, centerpiece, just so. Eric asked, "Is he getting help?"

"Doesn't want it," Mary replied. "Thinks he doesn't need it. He's wrong."

"Can't your parents make him go to one of those places?"

Mary shook her head, suddenly exhausted. It was a hard topic to discuss. "He's too old. Once you're eighteen, they can't legally make you do anything.

My mom says he has to be involved in the decision-making or it won't work."

"I'm sorry," Eric said, and he offered it up in such a way that Mary believed the words were genuine. It wasn't just an empty phrase. Eric truly felt sorry, as if he'd carried around some similar sadness of his own. Like he knew. What was it called? Empathy. Eric had something that people like Griff would never understand.

Everybody has stories, she figured.

"Thanks for telling me," he said. "I hope it gets better for you guys."

Mary pointed a finger at her heart. "Just don't tell anyone, okay?"

She caught herself and added, "Just to be clear, it's not because I'm ashamed or anything. It's just . . . you know. I don't need everyone in my business."

30
[denial]

EVERYTHING TURNED IN OCTOBER, THE MONTH WHEN it all hit the fan. Leaves were beginning to change color: yellow, orange, red. Mary had learned (and somehow remembered) the reason: in autumn, there was less light and temperatures fell, signaling to the trees that big changes were in the air. So they stopped making chlorophyll, like a factory shutting down, which was responsible for the green color. In colder climates, deciduous trees turned garishly brilliant before dropping their leaves altogether. Then they shifted into survival mode, like turtles overwintering in the mud. Skeletal limbs braced for whatever came their way.

Mary knew the feeling.

At home, Mary's mom sat in the backyard on a dark red Adirondack chair. Mary opened the sliding glass door. "Hey," Mary said, "there you are." She knew from the look on her mother's face that something was wrong.

"Tell me," Mary said.

"Oh, it's your brother again," Mrs. O'Malley said, glancing at her phone in irritation. "He's in love and moving in with his girlfriend, Vivian."

"Vivvy," Mary said, picturing the rail-thin girl who stood in their kitchen and tried to cook pizza while it was still in the box—and the plastic wrapper. Griff's sister. If left alone, she might have burned down the house. Great roommate.

"I don't have a good feeling about that girl," Mrs. O'Malley said. "I don't know what this new apartment is all about. He says he had a falling out with Dez, and that this new arrangement with Vivvy will save money. Supposedly there's other people living there, too." She bit at her nails, chewing on the skin of her fingers. "I'm at my wit's end."

Mary thought of making a joke about her mom's healing crystals. Maybe they weren't working out so well. Or maybe they were helping—she just needed to buy more! Maybe order by the truckload. Mary smiled to herself, imagining a huge delivery truck pulling up to the house. *Here's your quarry, lady, where do you want it?*

She decided not to share the joke. The time didn't seem right. "He's still going to the therapist?" Mary asked.

"Yes, so far, so good. But I don't know. It's so hard. You can relapse like that," Mrs. O'Malley said, snapping her fingers on the last word. "Jonny's so vulnerable right now. And he's smitten with this girl."

An hour later, mother and daughter were still in the yard, Mary reading in the hammock, when Ernesto returned home from the dealership. Yes, home. He was pretty much living there full time, along with his favorite iron skillet and kitchen knives. He surveyed the scene, the lack of movement in the kitchen, and proposed a solution. "Let's go bowling. We can get pizza there."

"What? Now?" Mrs. O'Malley said.

"Yes, now," Ernesto said, checking the time. "The

leagues start up at seven thirty on Fridays. If we get a move on now, there should still be lanes open. What about you, Mary? Want to come?"

Mary closed her book. "I guess—" she said without enthusiasm.

"You could bring a friend," her mother suggested. "I never hear about Chantel anymore."

"She's so busy," Mary replied.

Mrs. O'Malley stood with hands on her hips. Leaning left, leaning right. That was her notion of yoga.

"I'll try," Mary said to appease her mother. She sent Chantel a text: *I know this is random but do you want to go bowling? Like now?*

Shockingly, Chantel replied, *Sure!*

Okay, that wasn't expected.

Twenty minutes later, the four of them were trying on two-toned bowling shoes. Red and navy blue. "I look good in these," Mary observed.

"I'll order a couple of pizzas," Ernesto said. "Some wings, too. Soda okay? Root beer? What about you, Chantel, what floats your boat? How do you like your pie? Cheese, mushrooms, sausage, pepperoni, the works?"

"Just don't say Hawaiian," Mary advised. "Ernesto believes that pineapple on pizza is a crime against nature."

"Cheese, please," Chantel said. And to Mary, "Come on, let's go pick out our balls."

The two girls wandered off while Mrs. O'Malley and Ernesto set up camp in Lane 16.

"I was surprised you texted me," Chantel said.

"Yeah, I've been, like—"

"Busy, huh?" Chantel said. "Spending time with Alexis and Chrissie."

Mary didn't answer. She plugged her fingers into a pink-and-purple ball with a tie-dye design. It looked awesome but weighed a ton.

"I prefer a light ball," Chantel said, weighing the heft of a solid red ball in her hands.

Mary tried a green marble ball. It wasn't right, either. Also: not very pretty. "Oh wow, this one's cool!" She lifted up a bright neon orange ball.

Chantel was scowling, intently flipping through images on her phone. She held it out at arm's length to show Mary. It was an image of a heavy black girl in a bathing suit, from knees to neck. A silhouette of a pig's head sat on top of it. Below it were the words,

OINK, OINK! CHANTEL WILLIAMS WANTS TO MESS AROUND WITH YOU!

Whoa, that's messed up, Mary thought. Before seeing this image on Chantel's phone, Mary had remained in a twilight between knowing and not knowing. She'd been aware that stuff was going on without learning the details. But now seeing the hurt in Chantel's face, the impact hit home.

"You do this?" Chantel asked.

"What? Oh my God, no!" Mary sputtered. "Where'd you get that?"

Chantel's face was hard and resolute. She waited.

"Seriously, I swear," Mary said.

Chantel flipped through some images, but seemed to decide against sharing them. She pocketed the phone. "There are others that have gone around that are worse. Hakeem told me. He's disgusted by the whole thing. I'm surprised you haven't seen them."

Over Chantel's shoulder, Mary saw Tamara Agee and a few other girls from school enter the alley. *Please, no*, Mary thought. The last thing she needed was to be seen with Chantel. To Mary's relief, Tamara walked in the opposite direction.

"You have no idea what this is about?" Chantel's

eyes fixed Mary in place the way a pin through the thorax secures an insect to a display case.

"No," Mary said.

"I want to believe you, so I will," Chantel reasoned.

She knows who is behind it, Mary decided. *But she isn't sure about me.*

"Do you know who did this?" Mary asked.

"I have a good enough idea, but I'm not one hundred percent positive," Chantel said. "You know them. People you're friends with. I just ignore it. What am I going to do, take on the whole pack by myself?"

Mary raised an eyebrow, as if to ask, "Why not?"

"It's not who I am. I refuse to be shamed by them," Chantel said. There was steel in her voice. But in that brief moment, Chantel's guard dropped. Mary saw a sparkle of moisture in her eyes. Not yet a tear, but the pool from which tears are formed. Chantel said, "I can't get into trouble. My parents would take away my privileges."

"But you didn't do anything wrong."

Chantel wavered slightly. "Nobody's perfect, Mary. I'm not the angel you think I am. There are things I'd prefer my parents didn't find out. I'll handle this on my own. I just need it to go away."

"I hope it does," Mary agreed, uncomfortable with what she knew, and the dishonesty of her omission. She wasn't ready to face those truths.

Chantel looked back, pointed. "There's your mom, waving to us. Is this Ernesto guy her boyfriend?"

"Yeah," Mary said.

"You like him?"

They watched from a distance as Ernesto rolled a practice ball down the lane. He looked compact and surprisingly powerful for a short, stocky, elfishly bearded dude with pizza sauce (already!) on his shirt. The pins thundered into one another. A raucous strike. Ernesto gave up a hoot and performed a comic dance of joy with a big-time fist pump, causing Mary's mother to laugh out loud.

"He's okay," Mary said. But her thoughts were elsewhere. How did she get in the middle of something between Chantel and Alexis? They continued to pressure Mary to get involved in the next phase of their attack against Chantel. And Mary kept putting them off.

Why did she have to pick a side?

Mostly she wondered: *Was knowing—just knowing—a crime?*

31
[catch]

SOMEHOW MARY GOT ASSIGNED THE CRUMMY JOB OF raking the front lawn. Not all the leaves had fallen yet, so it struck her as a waste of time, like making a bed that you were only going to sleep in again later that same day. What was the point? She wore black jeans and an unbuttoned flannel over a long-sleeved tee. The raking was harder than it looked when other people did it. Mary felt an ache in the muscles in her arms and upper back. Good exercise, she decided, and an opportunity to think.

Chantel weighed heavily on her mind. It turned

out that Tamara did see them at the alley after all, so word got back to Alexis and Chrissie. They weren't thrilled with that news, though Mary did her best to downplay it. They still sat together at the lunch table. All seemed forgotten—until yesterday, when they came to Mary with a task.

A task? Maybe a test? They asked for Mary's involvement in "a little thing" they were planning for Chantel. While Mary raked leaves down to the curb, considering her options, she saw Eric walking a golden retriever down the street. It was curious, because Eric didn't live close by. Mary shifted her feet, placing her back to the boy, and kept piling up leaves.

And after a while, he said, "Hey."

What a surprise.

The dog strained against the leash, so Mary came forward to pet its head and shoulders. Eric told her that this one wasn't his. He walked dogs as a way to earn money. "You live here?"

"No, I just randomly rake leaves at strangers' houses," she deadpanned.

The dog, Ginger, looked thirsty. Mary ran inside to get her water. Maybe she just wanted Eric to linger a little longer. They sat down on the curb together, Ginger noisily lapping. "I haven't seen you hanging out with Griffin and Cody and those guys," Eric noted.

Mary tore at a maple leaf. "I'm trying to stay away from them. Too much weirdness."

Eric seemed to understand. He nodded in that thoughtful way of his, as if life were a Rubik's Cube to be puzzled over and solved. That if he could only think hard enough, and long enough, it would all fall into place. Ginger whined and Eric stood, reluctantly, getting ready to go.

"Do you want company?" Mary asked.

They walked through the suburban streets to the dog park, a fenced-in enclosure where Ginger could run free. Mary found an old tennis ball and hurled it. Ginger raced after it, thrilled beyond all reasonable measure. This was the most exciting thing in the world. A ragged old tennis ball. And every time one of them threw the ball, it was the most exciting thing in the world all over again.

Goldens weren't exactly rocket scientists.

"Good arm," Eric noted.

"That's right," Mary said, glad he noticed.

Her cell began to blow up with messages.

"Is something the matter?" he guessed.

Mary frowned, showed Eric the Photoshopped image intended to portray Chantel Williams. She confessed that Chrissie and Alexis wanted her to come over. "They want to get her back for liking the wrong boy."

"What are they going to do?"

He threw the ball. Ginger didn't move. She rested her chin on the cool earth, exhausted. Eric repeated his question.

Mary tucked back an errant strand of hair. How to explain it? "They are talking about making some anonymous web page. They want me to help. I'm good with computers."

"You've done stuff like that before?"

Mary nodded, feeling a tightness in her chest. "A little bit."

It was time to go, but Mary wasn't ready to leave Eric's side. That would have meant going back to her house, that big pile of leaves, and the choices and consequences she'd been reluctant to face. Besides, she liked being with him.

"So are you going over there?" he persisted. And

the way Eric looked at her—and waited for her answer—told Mary that her reply was important to him. Eric wanted her to say the right thing.

"No, I'm sick of it," Mary heard herself say, surprised at the bitterness that burned beneath her words. "Girls are the worst. We can be so freaking mean."

Eric asked if she wanted to go for pizza. And she totally did. They dropped off Ginger and went into town. It wasn't a date, whatever that was. Few people Mary's age knew what an actual date involved, though she guessed it was probably some combination of eating and chewing and awkward silences and kissing and teeth mashing together. Dates seemed like something from olden times. Getting a slice, on the other hand, wasn't strictly a boyfriend-girlfriend situation. It was just two people who felt like having a random slice of pizza, Mary told herself. Right? It didn't mean anything. But it was quietly exciting just the same.

They laughed about school and talked about different classes. Eric told her he was determined to try out for the modified basketball team, though not many seventh graders made it. He seemed, also, to have his own troubles. He talked about Griffin Connelly, troubled by recent events. Mary guessed that he was beginning to see Griff's dark side. She considered telling Eric about that day with David Hallenback, terrorizing that helpless boy with ketchup packets that scorching summer afternoon when they first met. She decided against it. "Let's not talk about him," she finally said. "That guy's not worth it."

"Cheers," Eric said, raising his strawberry Snapple.

He walked Mary all the way back to the front of her house. There was still some light left, the sun almost dropping behind the trees. Mary stepped inside and came back with a bag.

"Peanut?" she offered.

She didn't want to see him go.

"Um, seriously?" Eric said.

"I'm addicted," Mary said, immediately regretting the word choice. "It's ballpark food. Nothing better."

Eric took one peanut, crushed it between his thumb and forefinger, slid off the paperlike skin, and popped the nut into his mouth. He reached for more, and took a large handful.

"See what I mean?" Mary said. She dropped the

bag to her feet and plopped down, cross-legged on the October grass. "I got hooked at my brother's baseball games. My mother dragged me to every one, said it was important, you know, being a family. And I guess she bribed me with peanuts."

Mary unshelled a few while talking, never looking down, feeling them with her fingers. Soon there was a small mound of broken shells on the lawn, eight raw peanuts in her palm.

"Do you play ball?" Eric asked.

Mary shook her head. "Used to, softball. Pretty good, too."

Eric leaned back on his right hand, assessing her. "Shortstop?" he guessed.

Ha, Mary laughed. She jumped up, windmilled her arms, leaped forward, and executed the complex motion of a softball pitcher's underhand windup.

"Pitcher!" Eric said, clapping. "That's a hard windup. Do you have a spare glove and a ball? I'd like to see this in real time."

"Really?"

"Yeah, I do," Eric insisted. "Then I have to get going. My mom's probably wondering."

"Then she should get you a phone," Mary countered.

"True fact!" Eric said.

"Jonny's glove is probably in the garage somewhere. It's been a while. We throw all our sports crap in a big contraption."

"A contraption!"

"I don't know what to call it," Mary laughed. "It's just this big boxy netlike thing. Where we shove our stuff. Rollerblades and basketballs and Frisbees and whatever."

"Yeah, you're right, that's technically called a contraption," Eric said.

Mary skipped off and returned with a bright green softball and two gloves. She flipped a glove to Eric, who snared it midair.

They began tossing the ball back and forth. Finally Eric said, "Okay, let's see what you've got."

"I'm out of practice," Mary said, somewhat doubtfully. But almost in contradiction, she expertly paced off the distance, turned, and with a flattened hand gestured for Eric to squat in the catcher's position.

"Ready?"

Eric nodded. "Try not to hurt me."

Mary raised her glove just below her eyes, right hand on the ball. Her face was composed, relaxed, intent. She breathed in and the machinery started: her arms swung up and back, her hips came forward, her left leg pointed straight out, and everything leaped forward as the ball zipped from beside her right thigh, fast and true.

A perfect strike.

Mary couldn't keep the big smile off her face. It was, she decided right then and there, maybe the most beautiful pitch she'd thrown in her life.

"Nasty!" Eric took off the glove and blew on his hand, flexing his fingers. "I'm pretty sure it's broken," he joked, and tossed the ball back to Mary.

Mary snatched it with casual grace. "Now I'll show you my drop pitch. When it's on, I'm unhittable."

32
[apology]

DAYS PASSED. MARY DIDN'T GO TO CHRISSIE'S HOUSE or get involved in their plot against Chantel. She didn't do a thing. Lift a finger. Or say a word. Just stood by and let it happen.

Hoping, maybe, it would play itself out.

Not bad if you can live with yourself.

There's a tipping point in friendships, Mary had learned. It begins with a twilight stage, an in-between. During these past few weeks, Mary belonged and yet didn't belong. Her grip was slipping. She felt it in different ways, a million subtle signs: an expert eye roll, a whisper, a comment, a "like" on social media or not, a stinging insult accompanied with an insincere smile. It came down to inclusion and its opposite, exclusion. One example: everybody signs up for a club meeting after school on Tuesday, but Mary is the last to know. She can join the group—it's a free country, after all— but no one made the plan with Mary in mind. Come, don't come, whatever.

Mary was like a plane that was steadily losing altitude—engine two was malfunctioning and leaking gas. Still aloft, technically, but it wouldn't last. Only a matter of time before she hit the ground and burst into flames.

Mary could especially sense it regarding Chantel. Suddenly the hot topic wasn't discussed anymore. Or, at least, not when Mary was around. Maybe Alexis and Chrissie didn't trust her anymore. The hive brain understood before any individual person could articulate it: Mary still had a seat at the table, but she was out.

Summers never last.

And for Mary, the truth was, it felt fine.

Mary was ready to be her own person, no matter the cost. She also sensed trouble brewing for Eric. Something was going on between him and Griffin.

Mary didn't trust Griff, and now, for good reason, neither did Eric. She remembered what Griff said that day behind the middle school: "I told him that I was a good guy to be friends with, and a lousy enemy."

Even worse, she heard Sinjay and Pat goading on Cody the other day, saying he should take care of business with Eric. "We've got your back," Sinjay said. Mary made a decision to warn Eric to watch out. Don't trust any of those guys. Griff was a master manipulator. When he was pulling the strings, bad things were bound to happen.

Then last night the messages went out. Texts and emails and links, the whole social media onslaught— snarky, supposedly funny, pure nastiness directed at Chantel Williams. There was even a website dedicated to it. The source of the attacks was nameless, faceless. They'd done a good job covering their tracks. Tamara must have helped; she was smart that way.

Mary didn't sleep well that night, staring blindly into the darkness, and in the morning she stood before the bathroom mirror, facing the disapproval of her identical twin. Mary's face frowned at her reflection, visibly unimpressed—and, yes, she could see that by the fold of her arms and the cock of a hip. Mary turned to the smaller makeup mirror on the shelf. She leaned in close, flipped it for the intense, giant close-up. What was happening to her skin? Blotches, dry patches, blackheads. Stress, probably. She applied benzoyl peroxide to her face, washed and rinsed and dried, then rubbed in an oil-free moisturizer her mom had purchased. She scowled again at her twin's disapproving expression. *If you don't like it, do better,* the face in the mirror told her. Mary nodded at the message of her wiser twin. Do better, yeah, she'd give it a whirl.

In home base, third period, Mary overheard a couple of girls laughing about Chantel. It was all over school. The big joke. Mary fumed, her face contorted in anger. Tamara snapped back, "Like you're the innocent one. Keep your mouth shut."

Mary had to get out of there. She literally wanted to climb out the window. Fortunately, Mr. Scofield gave her a pass. Walking down the halls, Mary felt her whole body vibrate with anger and frustration.

By lunchtime, Mary had been ostracized. Dead girl walking. She'd lost her seat at the table. Not that Mary cared anymore. Being alone felt better than sitting with the wrong people. Not that it felt good. Her thoughts flashed on Jonny. Did he ever feel like this?

So sad and empty, like a plastic bag blowing in an alley, that he needed something to fill him up again? *Was that why he did it?* Mary gave sidelong glances at Chantel, who sat huddled with two friends. The way she sat, the expression on her face, everything about Chantel spoke of misery. She was hurting. Embarrassed and in pain.

Mary waited until lunch was over to talk to Chantel. To tell her the truth. Chantel was standing off to the side of the schoolyard, leaning against the building with a small group of friends.

"Chantel," Mary said softly.

One girl, Beatrice Rosario, stepped up in front of Mary, blocking her path. But Mary set her shoulders. She didn't budge. "Please," she said.

Beatrice looked back at Chantel, who nodded sharply.

Mary came forward. "I'm so sorry." She reached out a hand to touch Chantel on the arm, to connect, but Chantel pulled away. "Chrissie and Alexis—" Mary began, sputtering to explain, "No, I mean, me—I haven't been a good friend to you. I was silent when it mattered most—I didn't stand up—and I am so sad and so sorry."

Chantel listened, arms crossed, slouching against the brick wall, never looking Mary in the eye. After a while, Chantel's breathing became more regular, her emotions under control. She nodded once or twice. Scratched her arms. Finally, Chantel raised her chin and stood tall. "You hurt me very much, more than you'll ever realize—"

"Yes, I know, and I'm so sorry," Mary said. "But—"

"No, you don't get to talk," Chantel cut her off. "It's my turn to talk. You can listen, or not listen. I honestly don't care."

Chantel looked away, her head shaking. She lifted up a hand, made a waving gesture as if swatting away a fly. "Just . . . just . . . go. I've heard your words, Mary. But that's all they were. Just words. You're sorry. Okay, maybe you are. Good for you. Now go, leave me alone."

Mary hesitated.

Chantel turned away.

"You heard her," Beatrice piped up. "Go."

Mary looked at Beatrice. Nodded in defeat. This wasn't how she'd hoped her apology would play out.

"Wait," Chantel called. "Tell me why. Do you know? Why did they do this?"

Mary looked up. To the right, over the crown of trees, a mass of white cumulus clouds hovered, rimmed with sunlight. She imagined painting it, all the colors she'd need. Not just blue and white, but gray and silver, green, even yellow and pink. It would be nice to make something beautiful for a change. Four black crows landed in the open field, close to the tree line. The scavengers picked at something—a gray, dead squirrel. They pecked and ripped and hopped away, gulped and swallowed and butted in for another bite.

"Hakeem," Mary finally said. "I think it started with Hakeem."

"Hakeem?" Chantel repeated. "A boy? Those girls did this to me, all over some boy?"

A guttural sound came from Chantel's throat. A laugh, a screech of fury and astonishment. Mary knew she would hear that cry echoing in her ears for a long time to come.

"Time's up, buttercup," Beatrice said, leaning close and whispering in Mary's ear. "Now vanish."

Mary wished she could. Instead, she walked toward the doors. Still had half a day to go. Out of the corner of her eye, she noticed Eric standing alone.

He wore a puzzled expression on his face, which was typical of him. He was always trying to decipher meaning from the complex code of middle school behavior. She saw that he was watching a conversation between an unlikely pair, David Hallenback and Griffin Connelly, walking and talking close together, thick as thieves.

33

[rumor]

SOMEHOW MARY GOT THROUGH THE REST OF THE school day, a crippled ship drifting through rocky straits. The final bell blared, and they were released to the buses and bike racks, the sidewalks and coffee shops. The halls resounded with the metallic-gunshot clang of slammed lockers. Students raced off to the next thing. Sports practice, cheerleading, play rehearsals, band, chess club, LGBTQ meetings, the town library, a friend's house, the skateboard park, the shimmering universe inside their phones—a hundred urgent places to be.

Mary felt listless, lacking in all energy. She walked

absently toward the bike racks, forgetting that she had abandoned hers two weeks ago. Never a fan of the bus, she started to walk home. Out the doors, down the wheelchair ramp. In front of her, two girls chattered. Mary heard Azra talking about some dumb thing the boys were doing. A fight of some kind. Azra was telling Jamilah, a ringlet-haired girl with thick red glasses, and said, "Cody said he's going to teach that new kid a lesson."

Mary squeezed Azra by the elbow and guided her out of the path of departing students. "What new kid?"

Azra blinked her startled dark eyes, looked to Jamilah. "It's nothing," she replied, pulling her arm free.

"Please, Azra," Mary said. "I heard you. What new kid are you talking about?"

"The nice one, Eric Hayes. He's in our English class," Azra answered. "Cody said he's going to get him today."

"Today? When? Tell me what you heard," Mary insisted.

Azra nervously brushed hair from her face. "I don't know anything, just that Cody and some guys are out to get Eric. Something about an ambush."

"An ambush?"

Azra frowned. The sidewalk was thinning.

"We have to go, my father's waiting," Jamilah said, looking toward the cars that idled on the curbside.

"You don't know where or when?"

"Mary, that's all I know. But I think it was supposed to happen, like, now. After school," Azra said.

Mary knew she'd have to scramble to find Eric. Or Griffin. Anybody who might know something. She raced through the empty halls, footsteps echoing. Near the gym, she saw a boy reaching for the handle of the locker room door. "Hey," she called out, slightly winded, "are the guys from the football team in there?"

The boy, a broad-shouldered, dirty-lipped eighth grader who was attempting his first mustache, gave her a funny look. "That's right," he answered.

"Can you please see if Hakeem Downing is in there? I need to talk to him. I really appreciate it," she said.

"You his girlfriend?"

"Please, it's super important."

Hakeem came out two minutes later, dressed in black socks, white football pants, and a burgundy jersey, the number 56 stitched to his chest. He adjusted his shoulder pads. "You wanted me?"

Mary asked if he knew about the fight. Hakeem looked up and down the halls. "What I heard is that Eric called Cody a weasel, something like that. Talking behind his back. Cody found out about it."

"Is that even true?"

Hakeem shrugged. "Cody thinks so."

"I heard there's going to be an ambush," Mary probed.

"That's not me—I don't have anything to do with that stuff." Hakeem jerked a thumb, indicating the locker room. "Look, I've got to get ready for practice."

"Wait," Mary said. "Where will it be?"

Hakeem glowered, shaking his head. "What is it with everybody in this school? Haven't you had enough? Now you want to go watch a fight?"

"It's not like that," Mary said. "Please, Hakeem."

"I don't know where for sure," he answered. "Somewhere nearby, off school property. Check the cemetery first. I've heard people say they go there."

"Thanks," Mary said.

"You want my opinion? Don't get involved," he warned. "Whatever happens is going to happen. You'll only make it worse."

Mary hadn't gotten that far with her thinking yet,

didn't have a plan of action. She figured she'd improvise. "One last thing. Can I borrow your bike?"

Hakeem chuckled. "You are unbelievable, you know that? My goodness. You know the one, right? Diamondback, green frame. Combo is twelve, thirty-two, seven. Black lock. It better be waiting for me when I'm done with practice, five sharp."

"You're a good guy, Hakeem," Mary called out as she took off down the hallway. She whirled and cupped her hands around her mouth, still back-pedaling furiously, and bellowed, "For what it's worth, I'm on Team Chantel!"

Hakeem laughed and lifted his right arm, thumb up.

Mary found the bike—after searching the wrong rack for another heart-pounding ninety seconds—and zoomed past Officer Goldsworthy on her way out. He looked at her and his eyes lingered on the new bike. "Gotta fly!" Mary called. "Don't worry—it's Hakeem's!"

For an instant, Mary considered telling him about the fight. But her feet kept pedaling, making the decision for her. No time to lose.

34

[boot]

IT WAS ONE OF THOSE FACTS THAT EVERYONE IN TOWN knew, a random source of local pride: the Final Rest Pet Cemetery was the third largest of its kind in the United States. Adjacent to the middle school, it was sprawling with marble gravestones for cats and dogs. Mary guessed there were probably other types of pets buried there, too—because people absolutely loved their pets. Five minutes on YouTube could tell you that. And when those animals died, a part of their owners' hearts died with them. A decent burial and a $5,000 tombstone was the least they could do. Even for a pet iguana.

It felt disrespectful for Mary to zip around the gravel paths on a bicycle, but she had no choice. The grounds were empty anyway. She pedaled to a hill in the back, believing it would offer the best vantage point. Mary was right. Down below, she saw a group of seven boys: Cody, Sinjay, Will, Droop, Griff, Hallenback, and Eric. Two stood close together, Cody and Eric, engaged in a heated discussion. Cody's hand pushed against Eric's chest. The other five boys formed a ragged three-quarter circle around those two, spectators forming a noose. Cody drove a fist into the side of Eric's face. Eric rocked back, staggered, but was still standing.

Mary leaned forward, unsure of what to do next. Should she ride down? Try to stop it? Would they listen?

Or would that only make it worse?

Walk away, she silently urged Eric. *Don't fight back.*

And as if he'd heard her, Eric tried to do exactly that. He turned to walk away. Cody wasn't having it. He grabbed Eric by the shoulder to spin him around. Eric swung wildly, an errant roundhouse right, and Cody danced out of range, bouncing and weaving.

"Fight, fight!" the cries roared.

Mary could practically see a current of adrenaline shoot through the group. The boys were instantly energized by the action. They pressed closer, shouting.

"Do it, Cody!" Griff yelled.

And it was too late for Mary to do anything at all.

The fight was a mismatch, quickly finished. Two minutes, three minutes, tops. Eric defended himself to the best of his ability, but Cody was by far the more skilled fighter. In the end, Eric was on his hands and knees, spitting blood. Cody stepped back, looked at Griffin, made a final comment to Eric, and the boys all moved away. Satisfied customers every one. Except for David Hallenback, who moved closer to Eric. The freckle-faced boy pulled back his leg, swung forward, and planted his boot deep into Eric's stomach.

Eric crumpled to the ground, covering up his head with his hands, elbows tight together, pulling his knees into a protective ball. Hallenback kicked and kicked again, a spastic, uncoordinated rage that mostly failed to connect. It was as if a lifetime's anger poured into that chaotic assault. Every insult, every hurt he'd ever endured over a lifetime of hurts, fueled Hallenback's fury. Cody hurried back and pulled Hallenback away.

Even from the high hill, Mary heard Cody shout, "Leave him alone, Hallenback. He's down."

Helpless, Mary waited for the boys to leave. When they were out of sight, she rode down and braked beside Eric, who lay facedown on the grass. "Are you okay?" she asked, climbing off the bike. She heard worry in her voice, as if she didn't want to know the answer. For the first time Mary realized that she was scared.

She had feelings for this boy.

Eric slowly rolled over to look up. One of his eyes was already half shut, swollen and discolored. He squinted through the other one, lifting his head a few inches off the ground. He tried to smile, but it was unconvincing. A poor imitation. He mumbled something that Mary couldn't understand. She leaned close, touched him on the shoulder. "What?"

He let his head fall back on the cool earth, his one good eye staring up at the clouds. He breathed slowly and softly, open-mouthed. Felt tenderly for his ribs, grimaced. It seemed to Mary that while Eric was bloodied and bruised, he didn't appear to be seriously damaged. "I was hiding," she explained. "I watched from the hill." She wiped the hair from his face, touched him gently, and after a few more minutes she supported his torso and helped him sit up.

He gave a deep exhale. He spat. Just saliva, not blood anymore. A good sign. Eric looked at Mary questioningly.

"I've seen worse," Mary said, "but only in slasher movies."

He laughed like it hurt.

She helped him stand.

"Let's get you home."

35

[narcan]

VIVIAN CONNELLY NEARLY DIED ON A SATURDAY night in late October from an opioid overdose. By some measures, she did die. Her heart stopped. If not for the swift actions of a librarian at the town library and the emergency medical technicians who arrived a few minutes later, the Connellys would have been planning the funeral of their twenty-one-year-old daughter.

The next morning, a rainy Sunday, Mary's family gathered around the kitchen table. A visibly shaken Jonny recounted the events of the previous night. He looked ill, gaunt and rattled. He sat with his legs crossed, left arm wrapped awkwardly across his chest and his right hand free to run through his hair, pick at scabs on his face, or fidget nervously on the tabletop. He wore baggy, beltless jeans and a baseball tee and gray hoodie. Had he changed clothes since yesterday? Mary didn't think so.

"We scored that afternoon. Vivvy and I planned to get high together. There's that little park by the library we sometimes go to. It's a nice spot, you know, pretty and out of the way," he said, glancing at Mary. "We used to go there as kids.

"Saturday was our date night," he said without realizing the awfulness of what he'd said. "We always got really high on Saturdays . . ." His voice trailed away, abandoning the thought as if the sentence no longer interested him. He reached for a tall, thin glass of orange juice. Didn't lift it off the table, just turned it in his fingers. He spoke the next part directly to the orange juice glass, forehead knitted in concentration. "Vivvy was having trouble finding her veins, so I had to put aside my kit to help her. Otherwise it might have been me to take the first push. There was something wrong with this batch. We didn't get it from our regular source—maybe it was cut with fentanyl or rat poison or something, I don't know.

"After I gave Vivvy her dose, she smiled, so peaceful and beautiful, then her eyes got real big and she went sickly pale and slumped to the grass. I knew something wasn't right."

Mrs. O'Malley's hand found Mary's fingers beneath the table and squeezed, the two hands entwined, holding tight while their bodies sat rigid.

"I tried to carry Vivvy into the library, but her body was so floppy—I could barely lift her up. Her head kept lolling to the side. I stumbled and fell and kind of spilled her onto the lawn. I looked up and this woman came tearing through the front doors of the library, pulling on blue plastic gloves with her teeth as she ran." Jonny's body shivered from a sudden chill. He bit down hard on his lip. His words came faster now, more agitated, in droning, trancelike succession. "I was screaming, you know? Just screaming: 'Vivvy, Vivvy!' Out of my mind. The people in the library must have heard me.

"The woman pushed me aside and started asking me: 'Is this an overdose? Is this an overdose?' and I told her, 'Yes, yes, help her, please.' And she was at Vivvy's side and I saw her hands ripping open the Narcan kit, filling the needle from the vial—it was taking forever—and I'm just sitting there, holding my knees, yelling, 'Save her, save her!'—and she looks at me and says, as cool as you can imagine: 'You need to be quiet now, I have to concentrate if we want to save your friend,' and so I didn't say another word. I just shut my mouth and watched her jab that needle into Vivvy's shoulder. More people gathered around, somebody said the EMTs were on their way, and a man joined in. He gave her CPR and was saying, 'Come on, girl, come back to us, come on, come back to us.'

"It was like a chant, you know, or a prayer, whispering over and over, 'Come on, girl, come back to us, come on.'"

Mary felt like her fingers might snap off, her mother was squeezing so hard. She looked at Ernesto, and she saw that he was fighting back his emotions, lips a tight thin line, one finger tensely twirling his beard. Jonny looked totally distraught, so far lost into the memory of that scene that his eyes filled with horror, like he was staring into the face of some terrible beast.

Jonny said, "And the lady was getting scared, I could tell, because nothing's happening, so she said, 'I have another, I'm giving her another shot. Turn her, help me turn her,' and she's ripping open a new box. The man shifted Vivvy to her side, so now she's facing me and I can see her face. Totally lifeless, you know, like nothing I've ever seen before. Not sleep, not rest, not anything. It was just blank, empty. And this time the woman stabbed the needle into Vivvy's other shoulder. After a minute I could see her eyelids flutter like butterfly wings and open. Vivvy looked right at me, but I couldn't tell if she saw me or not. I don't even know what world she was in right then—I think maybe some land between life and death.

"She tried to sit up, but they were like, 'No, no, stay down, you've got to rest on your side in the recovery position,' and that's when the ambulance pulled up, and the cop cars, and the EMTs rushed up carrying bags and gear and they're pumping us with a hundred questions, all the details. It's like they had to know everything. Calling me 'sir this' and 'sir that.'

And that's when I saw Vivvy go away again, her eyes falling shut.

"They took out these paddles attached to wires like you see on doctor shows, and pulled up Vivvy's shirt."

"Defibrillators," my mother said.

Jonny nodded, yes, yes, that was the word. He leaned back in his chair, his face filled with something new, a kind of glow. "And this time it worked, and I could see everybody sort of relax, they could breathe, you know, and it didn't matter if they were cops or librarians or paramedics or people like me, we were all together on the grass. After a little while they carried Vivvy on a stretcher into the ambulance and took her away. I asked to ride with her, but they were like, 'No, sir, no, not happening.' They promised me she'd be okay."

"Thank God," Mrs. O'Malley said.

"That lady, from the library—"

"Mrs. deGrom," Mary's mother said. "She's the head children's librarian. She's been at the library forever. You might remember her, Mary."

Mary could picture the woman's face from story

hour and other programs geared toward young readers. Brown hair parted on the side, flecks of gray. Always wore big necklaces and colorful, dangly earrings. She didn't look like someone who'd be a hero.

Maybe heroes didn't have a look.

"I read about something like this," Ernesto offered, still running a hand down his wispy beard. It looked so tuggable to Mary, like a billy goat's. Ernesto said, "More and more public libraries are keeping a supply of Narcan on hand, just in case. One librarian in the article said she used to worry about overdue books, now it's overdoses."

"Times change," Mrs. O'Malley said. "Not always for the better."

Jonny listened politely. "She drove me to the hospital. That was nice of her. And then, I guess, she called you."

Mrs. O'Malley nodded, smiled at Ernesto. "I don't know how many red lights we ran getting there. Do you remember what you told us, Jonny, sitting in the waiting room?"

Jonny swallowed. He remembered. "I said, 'I'm ready, Mom. I don't want to live like this anymore.'"

Mrs. O'Malley tilted her head back, eyes closed, turned her neck from side to side. Mary could actually hear the grinding of the bones of her spine. She leaned forward, placed her two open palms on the table, reaching toward her only son, and asked, "Is it still true today? Are you ready to go to rehab and give it everything you've got?"

36

[never]

JONNY ANSWERED IN A SOFT, CLEAR, VULNERABLE
voice: "I'm ready, Mom. I'm ready."

Mary was happy to hear those words. It felt like
a winter wren had wriggled free from her heart, and
a feathery hopefulness filled her chest. Her mother,
on the other hand, did not show any joy. She simply
nodded with a serious expression. No smile. "Then I
think we need to act right away. I don't want to wait,
Jonny. I'll need to make some calls. I have a few con-
tacts. Finding a bed, and a place that accepts at least
partial insurance, won't be easy."

She rose to her feet, ready to get started.

"What about Vivvy?" he asked. "I love her, Mom. She's my soul mate."

"Oh, Jonny," Mary said, the words passed her lips before she could stop them. "You can't."

He scowled at his sister. "They released her already. She's back home."

"Is that true?" Mary asked her mother.

"That's the way it works," Mary's mother replied. "Some of these kids are back using that very same day. The system can't hold them."

Jonny hung his head and his shoulders heaved. "I don't know if she's using or not."

"You can't wait for her," Mrs. O'Malley said. "I know how much that hurts. I know you both care about each other. But Vivvy almost died last night. And it very easily could have been you."

Jonny never raised his head. "I know, I know." He shivered, rubbed his eyes. "It made me think of Dad."

"Oh?" Mrs. O'Malley said.

"Watching Vivvy's life drift away, it felt like Dad— just another thing I used to love slipping through my fingers."

Mary imagined the string of a helium balloon

running across a child's outstretched fingers until it was gone from reach. Off into the sky, the wild blue. She rose and went over to Jonny and wrapped her arms around him. She felt his body vibrate in her embrace, heart beating fast like a frightened rabbit's, a boy full of trembling sorrow. This was hard for him, too. Hardest for him, most of all. She didn't know what to say. No words could express what she was feeling. Instead, Mary just squeezed.

Eventually, Ernesto went into the living room, flicked on the television to a soccer game. Jonny followed him, stretched out on the couch, half watching while checking his phone, a fleece blanket pulled over the length of his body. Mrs. O'Malley shut herself away in the home office, making phone calls and occasionally letting out a groan of frustration that filtered through the closed door.

Mary remembered that she had a science test the next day. She went up to her room to study. She sat in front of a video review session on the computer, but her mind raced to distant galaxies. Oh well. It was only school.

Over dinner, Mrs. O'Malley announced that she

had secured a bed for Jonny in a rehab center in Minnesota. "I booked two plane tickets. We'll leave tomorrow morning."

Ernesto raised his eyebrows. "You two going to be all right?"

Mrs. O'Malley glanced at Jonny. Her eyes went back to Ernesto. She smiled. "If you drive us to the airport."

Jonny took the news without emotion. He seemed withdrawn, sullen. Skipping dessert, he went up to his room, acting neither happy nor sad. More resolute than anything. But pensive, also. It struck Mary that it was something he had in common with Eric, that deep-feeling quality. Tomorrow, Jonny had to face the biggest challenge of his life. And like a boxer before a fight, or Jesus before his arrest in the garden, Jonny wanted time to be alone to bargain with his fate. He said, "'Night," and shut the door.

IT STARTED TO RAIN THAT NIGHT, THE KIND OF VIO-lent downpour that pounds the houses and floods the streets. The winds thrashed and tree limbs crashed to the ground. A car alarm screamed down the street, blaring into the night. Dogs barked with madness. The electricity went out, power lines down.

"It's always something, isn't it?" Mary's mother observed, bringing up a battery-operated lantern for Mary's room.

Mary didn't get much studying done. Her thoughts fishtailed all over the place, like a car on an icy road. She raised the shades and opened her bedroom window, letting the angry wind and rain billow the curtains into her room. Emotions were like seasons, Mary mused. She accepted all the colors of the four seasons, the tender greens and deep blues, the brilliant oranges and the gray, washed tones of winter. Some people wished for endless summer, forever clear skies and sunshine. That sounded dreary to Mary. Monochromatic and dull. Things shouldn't always remain the same. That wasn't real life. She poked her head and shoulders out the window, leaning into the howling night to better know the storm. She thought of Jonny alone in his room, departing early tomorrow. If only she could learn not to love, if she could harden her heart, then the pain would diminish. It wouldn't hurt so much.

I hate loving you, she thought.

Mary had no choice, though she sometimes wished it otherwise: She loved her brother through and through. It's what made this year so impossible. But for now, for tonight, she wanted it no other way.

Mary knocked on Jonny's door and pushed it open. Jonny lay face-up in bed on top of the covers, one knee bent, hands hammocked behind his head. Mary walked softly on stocking feet, set the lantern light on low, placed it on the floor at the foot of the bed. Jonny shifted and with that movement wordlessly invited Mary to join him. They didn't talk for a long time. Just lay there together, wandering the pathways of their private thoughts. Eventually, he asked, "Don't you have a test?"

"I don't care. It doesn't matter," she told the ceiling.

Jonny turned, propped up on an elbow, looked at his sister. "You should care, May." He touched her nose with his finger. "You're so smart and good."

Mary didn't feel that way at all. But she nodded for him, not meaning it.

"Promise you'll do better."

"Sure," she said.

"You can't be like me," he said. "I have something

wrong inside of me, May. I don't know if I can be fixed. Promise me, May. Promise me."

Mary felt the warm pressure build behind her eyes, the tears beginning to come. To hide those tears, she reached her arms around Jonny's neck and buried her head in his knobby shoulder.

Her whisper came so softly that Jonny had to strain to make out the words: "I'll never give up on you," she promised. "Never, never ever. I'll never not love you, Jonny Bear."

37
[stones]

AT JONES BEACH, WHEN MARY WAS LITTLE, SHE USED
to beg her parents to try the coin-operated sight-
seeing binoculars on the boardwalk. They almost
always said no, explaining that they didn't have
enough quarters. Yes, she realized now, maybe there
was a faint remembrance of a fatherly presence in
those early memories—a jingling pocket with coins,
two hands lifting her up, strong thick tobacco-stained
fingers enclosed around her tiny rib cage. The binoculars didn't last long before time ran out, the machine
wanted to eat more quarters, and Mary had to squint
and shut one eye to see properly. She always felt des-

perate to see everything as quickly as possible. Most of all she marveled at the way she could spin the metal dial to focus. The picture would look all blurry and then, slowly, the scene came into crisp focus. Shapes, colors, details emerged with superhuman clarity.

That's how she felt about the past few months, from a lazy summer spent lounging at Chrissie's pool all the way into blustery November. Her blur period. It was strange to Mary how she could see a person many times, in dozens of different situations, and then suddenly *see* them. See them fully as they were, as if the metal dial turned and they became clear. For Mary, it was happening not only with Eric, but with everyone in her life. Griffin, Chantel, Alexis, Jonny, even Ernesto and her mom.

A new clarity.

When Ernesto started taking Zumba classes with her mother, Mary knew it was only a matter of time. For this was the act of a man hopelessly in love, because Ernesto in no way struck Mary as a Zumba class type of dude. He went because he loved her, that was all. Ernesto came home from the YMCA that past Saturday and popped open a beer while Mary's mother showered upstairs.

"Is that part of your Zumba training regimen?" Mary joked, nodding at the beer can.

Ernesto pressed three fingers against the back of his leg and grimaced. "That Zumba's no joke. I may have pulled a hammy."

"Are you the only guy?"

"There's another, but I've got better rhythm," Ernesto said. His expression changed, eyes lifted toward the ceiling, indicating her mother's bedroom. "I love her, you know. I'm going to ask your mother to marry me. I hope that will be okay with you."

Mary wiped her hands against her pants. Otherwise she stood as quietly as possible, unable to speak, but feeling the weight of the moment. Seeing the look of concern on his face, his earnestness, Mary smiled. "No, it's good. I'm just . . . wow. She'll be ecstatic."

"I don't know about your brother," Ernesto said doubtfully. "But Jonny will have to deal with it. Tough, right? This is our life. But he'll be okay. Don't you think?"

Mary answered, "He'll be fine."

She beamed at him, a wide, embarrassed smile.

Ernesto stood and took a half step toward Mary. He awkwardly lifted an arm like one raised wing, an invitation to embrace. Mary instantly walked into his arms with all her heart, their first hug as family. Ernesto was as excited and proud as a boy with a new kite. He showed Mary the ring. Then he took Mary by the shoulders, held her at arm's length, and said with great solemnity, "I'll be good to your mother, Mary, and also to you. That's my promise. I'm not a perfect man, but I'll try my best. I'll go to work, I'll do my job, I'll cook, fix things around the house . . ."

"I know, I'm glad," Mary said. "You've made my mom very happy. She was broken for a long time. It's time to feel whole again. When are you going to ask her?"

"Tonight," he told her. "We're going to a fancy restaurant. I have it all planned out."

The following day, Mary found three smooth, round, white stones on her pillow. On each stone was a hand-painted word: EYE, SEA, YOU. There was also an envelope addressed to Mary, which contained a note:

My Mary,

First off, please be assured that I didn't buy these at the mall. I found these beautiful stones at the ocean and they made me think of you. You are such a good, kind, upstanding young woman. No one is perfect. We all do the best we can. Mostly, I want you to know that I see you. I see who you are. And I'm so proud of the person you've become.

Love,
Mom

P.S. I borrowed your paints without asking, hope you don't mind!

Jonny sent a letter every week. He seemed to be doing okay, claimed that he was beginning to deal with his demons. He wrote that he was trying to learn how to love himself, a brand of self-help talk that Mary had never heard from him before. It didn't sound like him, but whatever worked. He wrote, *I think this is it.*

Like so many times before, she hoped it was true.

Experience had taught Mary to draw a line between optimism and hope. Optimism was the head, the intellect. You looked at something, analyzed the data, and decided there could be a positive outcome. Hope was something stronger. It came from the heart. No matter what happened, you never gave up hope.

Only Jonny could make it so.

38

[sticks]

AFTER THE FALLOUT FROM THE FIGHT, ERIC AND MARY created the "misfits table" in the lunchroom. For the time being, it was just the two of them eating together in social exile, but there was room for more misfits. Maybe one day they'd have a crowded table of friends who didn't belong to any clique or group.

Eric made the basketball team, which was amazing. Just him and one other seventh grader in the whole school. Their first practice scrimmage against another school was scheduled for that afternoon. Griffin's table had a new member, David Hallenback, which was just too weird for words. Pretty sad, actually, because nobody over there actually liked him. One day, Mary watched as Hakeem got up from Griff's table, walked right past Alexis and Chrissie without a look, and came to sit beside Mary, across from Eric. "You guys look so damn lonely," he joked, grinning.

He told Eric that his father knew a guy who knew a guy, and somehow he got free tickets to see the Nets in Brooklyn next weekend. Against the Lakers.

"Cool," Eric said.

"So do you want to come?" Hakeem asked.

"Wait, you're asking if I want to see my first NBA basketball game ever in my life? Seriously?"

That was pretty great, Mary thought. The smile on Eric's face. And, yeah, the way he jumped around ecstatically. His happy dance.

Best of all, Chantel started coming by the table. She didn't sit, but lingered for a few minutes. Mary knew it was mostly because of Hakeem, but Chantel sent little signals that all was forgiven, if not ever forgotten.

"I never told you," Mary said, "how much I love that your mother calls you Chanti. It's so sweet."

"Chanti? I never heard that," Hakeem said, "I like it, too! Chanti, Chanti," he sang in a warm, rich voice.

Chantel blushed, delighted.

Mary pointed at Eric's supply of Double Stuf Oreos. "You going to eat those, or are they just going to sit there?" She didn't wait for a reply. It wasn't that kind of question.

After the last bell of the school day, Mary waited by Griffin Connelly's locker. She stood with her back against it, arms crossed, one knee bent. He saw her from a distance, but failed to muster his usual swagger.

"What?" he said as if letting out a groan.

"Can we talk?"

"We are," he said. "This is talking."

Mary shook her head a little sadly. "Not here."

"What about?"

"You know," Mary said. "Vivvy."

With a flick of his fingers, Griff gestured for Mary to step aside. He spun the dial, stuffed some books into his backpack, turned around. "Where to?"

Mary led him behind the school, past the court and track, up a path into the woods to where they had biked together on a scalding summer day that felt so long ago. She had not been to that spot since. There were still ketchup packets on the ground, along with other accumulated litter. Mary pulled out a kitchen trash bag she had brought from home for this purpose and started to clean up. Griffin watched her, unmoving. After a while, he picked up a plastic soda bottle and dumped it in the bag. Not a lot of help, but it was something.

"How's your sister doing?" Mary asked.

Griffin paused—he breathed in, he breathed out—and worked very hard to hide any emotion. But his eyes darted about, unable to fix on any object. He looked down. And his hands lifted in a sort of helpless shrug. He didn't know.

Mary waited him out, refusing to fill the empty space with words.

He said, "She's . . ."

Griff looked up, and in that instant Mary saw a different boy than she'd seen before. The surface toughness melted away. The anger, the cruelty. Beneath it all he was merely a boy who was lost: vulnerable and shaken. He reflexively blew the hair from his eyes and wiped the side of his face with a closed fist. "I don't know, Mary. She's home, I guess, doing what she does."

"Home?"

"Her apartment," Griff clarified. "My father refuses to speak to her. Doesn't want me to, either. He says it's tough love. He says . . . all sorts of things. But I don't hear much *love.*"

"Have you tried to contact her?" Mary asked. "Secretly?"

Griff looked to the gray, cloudless sky, the leafless trees, the grass that had lost its deep green. He closed his eyes and shook his head.

"She almost died," Mary said.

Griff bent to pick up a stray ketchup packet, crumpled it in his fist. "I know," he said so softly that Mary almost didn't catch the words.

"Are you okay?" she asked. Mary stepped forward, but caught herself. She wanted to console him, embrace him, offer him strength, but it wasn't her place to do that for him. She held back and watched.

"What am I supposed to do?" he said, wheeling around. "You want me to cry, Mary? Is that it? You ask if I'm okay? Yeah, sure, I'm fantastic. Nothing bothers me. That's her problem, right? I'll be fine."

"Griff," Mary said. "My brother was there, you know. He says he loves her."

Griff picked up a thick fallen branch. He weighed the heft of it in his hands like a ballplayer. It looked like a weapon in his hands, and for a moment Mary wasn't sure what he intended to do with it. With a fluid motion, Griff violently slammed it against the nearest tree truck. *Crack*, it snapped in two, the broken half flying into the thicket.

Griff dropped the stick, bent over with his hands on his thighs, shuddering in the echo of that blow.

Mary cast her eyes around. What else could she do? They had gotten most of the litter. "Jonny's in rehab now. Did you know that?"

Griff glanced up, shook his head. "I don't know a lot of things, Mary," he said. "So many things. Haven't you figured that out yet?"

"You could call her. Send a card. Something."

Griff shook his head again. "It's not like that. You wouldn't understand. My father says she's hopeless anyway."

"Don't listen to that," Mary said. "You have to hope, Griff. Things can change. She can change."

Griff looked at her with doubtful eyes.

"And you can change, too, Griff," Mary said, the words barely getting past her constricted throat and lips.

Griff frowned, turned his back to her. Maybe he couldn't look her in the eyes. It was getting late. Mary had planned to watch the modified basketball game. Be there for Eric. She checked her phone. "We should go."

Griffin shrugged and sank down at the base of the tree. He looked tired and defeated. "You go, I'm gonna stay."

"You sure?"

Griffin laughed, a short choking sound. "Sure, I'm sure," he said. He picked up a stone and flicked it away.

Eye. Sea. You.

"If you need anything," Mary offered, "I'll be around. Just to talk or whatever. Okay?"

He didn't answer.

"I hope she, you know, gets the help she needs," Mary said, and turned to walk away.

After a downcast minute, Mary lifted her chin and quickened her pace. She walked faster, her stride longer, more purposeful. She checked her phone again, 4:13. The game was supposed to start soon. Eric said he probably wasn't going to start. It didn't matter to Mary. She wanted to be there in the stands. He deserved it, and so did she. A reason to stand and cheer.

Mary broke into a run and never looked back.

Author's Note

ON SCHOOL VISITS, AND IN FAN MAIL, I'VE REPEAT-
edly told readers that no, thanks very much for asking, but I had zero intention of writing a sequel to
Bystander.

I felt that the book was complete and self-
contained. There were hints and suggestions for what
might happen after the last page; I was content to
leave those imaginings up to each individual reader,
where they belong.

So what changed?

It was a subtle shift. I'd been stuck in one way of
thinking: that a sequel would be about what happens

next. Then it dawned on me that I could tell Mary's story—a minor but crucial character in *Bystander*. In fact, I could tell much of Mary's story that occurred *before* the events that took place in the previous book. Here I'd catch up to that time line, overlap slightly, and take at least one step beyond.

That is: prequel and sequel.

And a story that stands alone.

I discovered an important distinction: not a longer story, but a *larger* one. The canvas got bigger.

Everyone has stories. Most of us have no idea what others are going through. We move through our lives, running into people all the time, and we just don't know what is really happening behind closed doors. So that's where it started for me. I asked myself, *What's been going on in Mary's life?*

My editor, Liz Szabla, was enormously helpful during a couple of long conversations that explored the possibilities. It hit us that Mary's brother had a substance use disorder, though I'm sure I would not have known to use that specific language at the time. I had a lot to learn.

Fortunately, there's a wealth of informative, raw, deeply personal literature on the subject. I should mention, in particular, six books that were especially enlightening: *If You Love Me* by Maureen Cavanagh; *Beautiful Boy* by David Sheff; *Saving Jake* by D'Anne Burwell; *Addict in the Family* by Beverly Conyers; *The Joey Song* by Sandra Swenson; and *Beyond Addiction* by Jeffrey Foote, PhD, Carrie Wilkens, PhD, and Nicole Kosanke, PhD, with Stephanie Higgs.

It was painful reading at times. I didn't write for months. Just took notes and thought and thought. The stories I encountered were remarkably inspirational, ultimately leaving me with a feeling of awe and respect. My empathy for "the addict" deepened, and the more I learned, the more I felt a sense of clarity about what I needed to say about this hidden disease that is all too frequently associated with blame and shame.

Years ago, on a school visit, I met a librarian, Colleen Leclair, who shared with me some of her experiences as a mother of a young man with substance use issues. We've stayed in touch ever since, and she's been generous and open with her hard-won insights.

I'd also like to thank Young Do, Executive Director of Hospitality House in Albany, New York.

A counselor had suggested that I contact Young, who instantly agreed to meet for coffee. He was amazingly open and supportive. Young and I talked for nearly two hours. He invited me to visit his facility, and he's been a source of inspiration and guidance throughout. In fact, a story that Young confided about his own experience gave me the inspiration for the opening of *Upstander*.

The narcan incident described in the book sprang from further reading and conversations with librarians. Of course, it's something many of us have known all along. There are heroes out there, and some of them are working in our public libraries, doing whatever it takes to better serve the needs of the community.

In the world of substance use, treatment strategies are openly debated. No one has the blueprint solution. Every situation is unique. But I have come to believe, more than ever, that unfailing kindness and love and connection are essential elements for successful recovery. At least, I think that's the best place to start—with an open, fragile, resilient heart.

And never, ever give up hope.

Thank you for reading this Feiwel & Friends book.

The friends who made

UPSTANDER

possible are:

Jean Feiwel, Publisher

Liz Szabla, Associate Publisher

Rich Deas, Senior Creative Director

Holly West, Senior Editor

Anna Roberto, Senior Editor

Kat Brzozowski, Senior Editor

Dawn Ryan, Senior Managing Editor

Kim Waymer, Senior Production Manager

Erin Siu, Associate Editor

Emily Settle, Associate Editor

Rachel Diebel, Assistant Editor

Foyinsi Adegbonmire, Editorial Assistant

Michael Burroughs, Senior Designer

Lelia Mander, Production Editor

Follow us on Facebook or visit us online at mackids.com.
Our books are friends for life.